Erotica Short Stories, Vol. 15

MY
WOMAN'S
Dirty Secrets

JUST PLAIN BOB

WARNING

This book contains sexually explicit scenes and adult language. It may be considered offensive to some readers. This book is for sale to adults ONLY.

Please store your files wisely where they cannot be accessed by underage readers.

About the Publisher

4Fun Publishing, a member of **BLVNP Incorporated**, 340 S. Lemon #6200, Walnut CA 91789, info@blvnp.com / legal@blvnp.com
NOTE: Due to the highly emotional reaction of some people to works of erotic fiction, any email sent to the above address that contains foul language or religious references is automatically deleted by our anti-spam software and will not be seen. All other communications are welcome.

DISCLAIMER

Erotica Short Stories, Vol. 15

My Woman's Dirty Secrets

By: Just Plain Bob

Table of Contents

Joan's Baby

I hated the holidays. I didn't use to, but for the last three years they had been hell for me. Actually, it wasn't the holidays so much as it was my mother. Don't get me wrong, I don't hate my mother, but I did hate being around her. She lives far enough away from me that for most of the year my only contact with her is by phone. When I'm on the phone and she gets on her kick I can hang up, but when she visits over the holidays and the contact is up close and in person, I can't get away. Her kick?

"When are you going to have kids? When are you going to give me grandbabies? Jesus, Joan, you have been married six years now and it is time for you to start a family. I want grandchildren."

At first I was able to put her off by telling her that Donny and I had decided not to have kids until we were financially stable and that we had some places we wanted to go and some things we wanted to do before we settled down and started a family. It was our third anniversary when she started hacking on me.

"Donny has a good job, you are in your own home now, and I want grandbabies while I'm still young enough to enjoy them"

The problem I had with that was that I was just the opposite. I was still young enough to want to have some life before I saddled myself with kids. I couldn't tell my mother that, so I lied.

"We are trying mother, it just hasn't happened yet."

It was the wrong thing to say because at least once a week after that she would ask if anything had happened yet and I would say no, that we were still trying. This went on for about six months and then she started giving me advice on things I could do that would increase my chances of getting pregnant. I would say that I would try them and in the next phone conversation I would tell her that I had, but that so far nothing was happening.

I got to where I dreaded talking to her on the phone. I bought myself a brief respite one day when I lost it and went off on her. I was having a bad day anyway and when the phone rang and I answered it and heard my mother say "Hello Joan" I just said, "Good morning mother and no, I am not pregnant." Then we got into an argument and I told her that it seemed like the only reason she ever called me was to see if I was going to have a god damned baby. We didn't talk for weeks after that.

But the holidays were the worst. Mom always came the week of Thanksgiving and stayed until the day after Christmas. You can always hang up the phone on someone, but how do you hang up on someone sitting across the table from you? Grandbabies, grandbabies, the grandbabies are all I listened for hours on end.

My mother was constantly on the subject and always saying things like, "When I was your age I already had you and Sarah (my sister) and I'm here to tell you that the older you get, the harder it is to raise a child. You need to start your family now."

The mention of my sister Sarah always pissed me off. I both hated Sarah and envied her and both for the same reason – she didn't have to put up with the shit from mom that I did. On Sarah's twenty-first birthday mom asked her when she was going to settle down, get married and start having kids. Sarah said, in front of all the guests at her birthday party, "I'm not. I'm gay and my significant other and I have no plans to adopt." What that did of course has pushed all of my mother's attention off onto me.

Donny and I had been married seven years when I finally decided that the time was right to have children. I talked it over with Donny and he seemed reluctant, but he said, "Okay, if that's what you want." The gods must have decided to make me pay for all the lies I told my mother because a year and a half went by without my getting pregnant. I even did all the things that my mother had suggested back when I was faking it and nothing happened. I went in and had myself tested and was told that I should have no trouble conceiving and bearing a child. I asked Donny to get tested and a week later he told me that he had been tested and that he had a high sperm count.

"It will happen honey, we just have to keep trying."

We did keep trying and nothing happened. We would have kept on trying with nothing happening for years if I hadn't run into an old friend from school one day while grocery shopping. Gwen and I had gone to community college together and we had kept in touch. Not really close touch, but we exchanged Christmas cards and talked on the phone half a dozen times a year. She had gotten her degree in nursing and had gone to work for a clinic. We left the grocery store and went a Denny's to have lunch and talk. Halfway through the meal she said, "Can I ask you something really personal?"

"I guess so, but I don't promise to give you an answer."

"If you don't, you don't, but I'm curious so I'll ask anyway. How is your love life?"

It wasn't what I expected and I hesitated a moment or two before deciding to answer. "It is fine."

"Good. I was worried about it. You know men, they have such fragile egos when it comes to their manliness that they will sometimes lie."

"I don't understand. Why the question and why were you worried and what were you worried about?"

"Just curious is all. Donny says your love life is great every time he comes in for his check up and to get his shot, but I never knew whether he was lying or not. Not everyone in the male contraceptive program tells the truth and that skews the data. We know for a fact that the side effects of the Cocktail – that's what we call it, "The Cocktail" – can have a limiting effect on male erection in about four percent of the sample. But that number could be lower or higher depending on the truthfulness of the program volunteers. When Donny came in and volunteered for the program he told us that you had a great sex life and you have maintained a great sex life. I was just curious."

No more so than I now am, I thought as I said, "Donny never did tell me much about the program other than that he had volunteered because of the problems that I was having with the pill."

"Well, like I said, we don't have an official name for it yet, but the cocktail is a mixture of synthetic testosterone and progestin and it is supposed to inhibit the production of sperm in the male."

"I guess we can assume that it is working with Donny and me, but how about others?"

"So far it has proven to be about eighty percent effective."

"So you do have failures?"

"Oh yes, and we make sure that the volunteers are aware of that fact. In fact, we make them sign a waiver acknowledging it."

I walked away from my lunch with Gwen mad enough to kill. That bastard! That miserable bastard! "Sure honey, okay, whatever you want" and all the time he was a volunteer in a male contraceptive program. There I was, trying everything I could think of to get pregnant – I even stood on my head after making love so the sperm would flow down to the egg – and Donny was doing his best to see that it never happened. I was mad! I was fucking furious and if Donny would have been there just then I would have done him some serious bodily harm. I was so mad I stopped at a bar to get a drink and calm me down.

I was sitting at a table sipping a vodka tonic and making plans to castrate Donny when I got home when I heard, "Joan baby, long time no see."

I looked up and saw Harry, an old boyfriend of mine. Actually, he was an old lover. Harry was the second man I'd ever had sex with. "Mind if I join you?" and I told him to go ahead. Six drinks later I was on my back on a bed in the Bide-A-Wee Motel as Harry tried to make up for the eight years he hadn't seen my pussy. It was my first time being unfaithful to my husband, which kind of shows just how pissed at him I really was.

Harry fucked me four times that afternoon and we were getting dressed to leave when he asked if he could see me again. I was on the verge of saying, "No Harry, this was a mistake, a pleasurable mistake, but a mistake, just the same" when a thought hit me – what if Harry had gotten me pregnant? Wouldn't that just serve Donny right! Donny already knew that there was a twenty percent failure rate in the program he was on. Yeah, why not.

"I'd like that Harry, but you can never, ever contact me, so give me a number where I can reach you."

He gave me his number and for the next two months Harry and I tried to fuck each other to death. We met three or four times a week during the day and I met him on Tuesday nights when Donny went bowling, but as much sperm as Harry shot into me I still didn't become pregnant. By that time I was determined to have a baby and since Donny and Harry had not produced I looked around for other old boyfriends or old lovers. By the end of the year I was juggling seven guys, counting Donny and Harry, and I had never been so sexually satisfied in my life, but I still wasn't pregnant.

Then one afternoon I was having lunch with Harry prior to an afternoon session at the Bide-A-Wee.

"I played cards with a bunch of guys last night."

"Oh? Did you win or lose?"

"Depends on the way you look at it."

"That's a strange answer."

"Yeah, well, you know how guys are, they like to brag about their sexual conquests."

"Yeah, so?"

"Well, first John bragged about how he was fucking you and then Art chimed in and said he was fucking you which made Mark laugh and we asked him what he thought was so funny he said he said, "I wonder how she manages it. I'm getting some too. She must spend most of her day on her back. We are all getting each other's sloppy seconds and never knew it." I didn't mention that we were getting it on. So, is it true? Are you doing all of us?"

What the hey, I was caught so I admitted that it was true. Then Harry wanted to know why.

"Did something change you into a nymphomaniac?"

"No, I'm just trying to get myself pregnant."

"That's what husbands are for."

"Some maybe, but not mine" and I told him the whole story.

"You don't care that you would be sticking him with somebody else's kid?"

"What I am trying to do Harry is having a child. I'm the one who will stay at home and raise it. I want a baby and Donny is lying to me telling me he is trying hard to knock me up. The bottom line is that he will never know. Besides, it might end up being his. The program he is in, has a twenty percent failure rate. Add to that the holidays are fast approaching and I don't want to go through another holiday season listening to my mother whine about when am I going to give her grand kids."

Then Harry wanted to know if I knew when I would be most fertile and did I track temperatures and all that and I told him that I did.

"Next time you are fertile we will see to it that you get pregnant."

"We?"

"Trust me on this one sweetheart, you won't be disappointed."

A week later, on a Monday, I called Harry and told him that the charts showed that Wednesday was going to be my peak time that month.

"Meet me at the Bide-A-Wee at noon tomorrow and plan on staying there as long as possible before you have to go home to Donny."

That night at dinner, I told Donny that he wouldn't be going to bowling Tuesday night. "You are going to spend Tuesday, Wednesday, and Thursday nights between my legs and we will get the job done."

"But honey, we are in a run for first place and I need to be there."

"Tough shit Donny. You will be here tomorrow night or the only holes you will be sticking your dick into will be the three drilled into your bowling ball."

Hey, he at least deserved a chance at being the daddy even if he had been screwing me around.

I was at the motel at eleven-thirty and Harry was already there waiting in the parking lot. He went in and got us a room and five minutes later he was between my legs and going for glory. He was in mid-stroke when there was a knock on the door and he stopped and pulled out of me which set me off screaming at him.

"God damn it Harry, I was almost there. What the fuck are you doing leaving me hanging like this?"

"Just hang on sweetheart, you have all afternoon."

He answered the door and John and Art were standing there. Harry let them in and they started undressing.

"What the hell is going on here Harry?"

"What is going on sweetheart is that we are going to keep a cock in you all afternoon and we intend…" and there was another knock on the door interrupted him. He opened the door and Mark was standing there with two other guys that I'd never seen before. Harry stepped aside and let the three into the room and then closed the door.

"As I was saying, we are going to keep a cock in you all afternoon and pump so much sperm into you that you will slosh when you walk. We will do the same thing tomorrow and Thursday and if that doesn't get you pregnant, then you may as well assume that the gods don't want you to raise a kid. Okay, you know John, Art and Mark, but you have never met Bill and Steve. They are friends of mine and I vouch for them. I asked them to join us for the next three days because of their history. Bill has six kids and his wife swears that all he has to do is look at her and smile and another one is on the way. Steve has seven kids and his wife won't even let him touch her anymore unless she has her diaphragm in, he has a condom on and he pulls out before he cums. Since I didn't clear this with you ahead of time all that has to happen now is for you to say yes."

I looked around the room at the six men. It was a big step for me. I'd never been with more than one man at a time before, but then I considered that the holidays were coming and with them my mother and I did want a baby. I took one last look around the room and then spread my legs wide, "Gentlemen, start your engines."

I looked around the room at the six people and smiled to myself and then I said, "This is a very special Thanksgiving for me. I'm thankful that I can announce that I'm pregnant and that there will be another chair at this table next year"

The range of emotions from the others at the table was mixed. My mother was overjoyed of course. Sarah and Milly (her 'significant other') had looks of "Oh, you poor sap" on their faces and Donny's parents were congratulatory, but Donny was stunned. I smiled at him, but he didn't smile back.

"I saved the announcement for today sweetie because I wanted it to surprise you."

"Well, you certainly did that."

Did I feel bad about doing that to Donny? Not at all. I wanted a baby and I got one and there is one chance in seven that the baby is his. He did make love to me a total of sixteen times over the three days and nights when the other six were fucking me. Oh, I'll admit that the odds are nowhere near one in seven, but my math skills are not nearly good enough to figure out the real odds. Take Donny's sixteen times, factor in the twenty percent failure rate of the contraceptive program, add the number of times six other men had made sperm deposits in me over the same three day period and only God could come up with the real odds.

I had a beautiful nine pound baby boy and I named him Donald Evans Marcus, Junior. Am I going to get a DNA test to find out who the real father is? No. It doesn't matter to me who the father is, the baby is mine and that is all that matters, at least to me.

My last day as a round-heeled slut was the day after the doctor confirmed that I was with child. I called all the guys and thanked them for their efforts and then I met them at the Bide-A-Wee for a celebration. Following that I was loyal to Donny for the next three years, right up to the day he left me. And no, it had nothing to do with the baby. Donny left me for a secretary who works where he works. She was ten years younger than me, had bigger boobs and god knows what else.

Life got real interesting after that. Was I pissed? Hell yes, but even as pissed as I was I wasn't a total bitch. Since Donny had obviously not wanted to be a father and was only a so-so daddy after the baby came, I cut him a deal. Instead of selling the house and splitting the proceeds he signed the house over to me, I didn't ask for alimony and we never mentioned little Donny in the divorce papers so he didn't have to pay child support.

My mother moved in with me and became my live-in babysitter

and I went back to work. One year after the divorce, I began dating again and Harry found out and started coming around. We dated several times and then started keeping steady company. He keeps after me to make the arrangement permanent and I was considering it when something totally surprising and unexpected occurred. Donny's relationship with his husband stealing bimbo cratered and he came home begging for forgiveness and asked me to take him back.

Interesting situation that. I loved him and I was crushed when he left me and since he'd been gone, I don't believe a day went by that I didn't think of him. That put me between a rock and a hard place because I had developed some pretty strong feelings for Harry.

"You can't seriously be thinking of taking him back," said Harry, "Especially after what he did to you."

"I don't know Harry, maybe that was Fate's way of seeing to it that I got my comeuppance for what I did to him."

"But he did it to you out in the open in front of God and everybody. He doesn't have any idea of what you did."

"I didn't say that HE did it to punish me Harry, I said maybe it was Fate's way."

I don't know what I'm going to do yet. I'm in the position of going steady with Harry, but I'm dating Donny as I try to figure out what to do. A weird relationship to be sure, but one with unique benefits – my sex life is outstanding what with two men after me. I may not ever make a decision if I can keep both of them hanging around.

End of the 1ˢᵗ Story

Ada's Cuckold

"Jerry?"

"Yes, dear?" "Would you come in here please?"

"Yes, dear, right away."

I hit the stop button on the remote to stop the movie I was watching and then went upstairs to the bedroom. My wife Ada was lying on her side fondling the cock of the black man lying next to her.

"Roy has just finished some very energetic fucking and he is thirsty. Would you please get him something to drink?"

"Yes, dear. What would you like, Ray?"

"Just water would be fine."

"With ice?"

"No, that won't be necessary."

"Okay, one glass of water coming up" and I headed for the bathroom.

As I headed for the bathroom, I pondered, and not for the first time, what it was that caused human beings to do the things they do. What was it that caused people to do things so far out of line with their character? Here I was, a man who considered himself a 'manly man' and I was running around saying "Yes dear" to my wife and waiting hand and foot on the smirking black asshole who was fucking her. Is this where I expected to be when Ada and I married? Hell no! So why was I smiling and doing things that went so far against my basic nature? What was the thing that caused me to be everything that I didn't want to be? Well, in my case it was greed. Pure unadulterated greed.

I had married Ada for her money. Ada had married extremely well when she had finished college and ten years later when her husband was killed in an auto accident, Ada found herself very, very wealthy. She was a great looking lady and very sexy, but make no mistake - I'd have gone after her if she was as homely as hell and as fat as a pig. She had money and I had been dirt poor all my life and I would not have let a little thing like looks get in the way.

<<O>>

I had graduated from college with a degree in Business Management and had gone to work, but I wasn't making the kind of money I wanted fast enough. I'd made it to college on scholarships, but it had still taken student loans to help get me through and what with living expenses and paying back those loans I never seemed to have much left. I was out looking for ways to augment my income and a friend suggested that I might be able to make a few bucks as a club fighter. I had done pretty well for myself in Golden Gloves competition and I found that I could get two, maybe three fights a week. I knew that I wasn't good enough to ever make it to the main event, but I could do all right in the three, five and seven round pre-lims. It was at one of those pre-lims that I met Ada. She was in the front row with several of her girlfriends the night I fought Ripper Washington. I found out later that she was there on a dare. Anyway, I happened to look down at her and saw her looking up at me, I winked and gave her a thumbs up and she laughed, waved and gave me a big smile.

Ripper was a big black dude, built like a tank, and the book on him was that he was a plodder. No fancy footwork, just walk into you and wear you down until you were too tired and then he'd nail you. The bell rang for the first round and I danced out and met Ripper in the middle of the ring and my first punch was a left jab that skipped past his guard and hit him dead on the chin. It was a lucky punch and I knew it, but it was a lucky punch that dazed him enough to cause him to drop his guard and a right cross put him down for the count (I met him six months later in a five round pre-lim and he damn near killed me). I danced around the ring with my hands in the air and I saw Ada jumping up and down cheering. An hour later when I came out of the dressing room, I found her waiting for me (again, on a dare) and I asked her to join me for a cup of coffee. She accepted and soon we were dating and we seemed to get along well together. Then I found out she was rich and I put on a full court press. Nine months later we were married and settled down to live happily ever after.

Happily ever after turned out to be two years, four months and eighteen days. I came home one night to find Ada dressing to go out.

"We are going somewhere?"

"Not we, just me," she said as she rolled on her nylons and clipped them to her garter belt.

"What's the occasion?"

"I need a change," she said as she slipped on a pair of black

CFMs.

"A change from what?"

As she slid into a little black cocktail dress she said, "We've been married for what, almost two and a half years now?"

"Yeah, about that."

"Well, I think it is time for me to sample another cock."

"You what?"

"I'm going out looking for something strange tonight. If I find something I like, I'll probably bring him home with me so you will have to sleep in one of the spare bedrooms tonight." She looked over at me and said, "Close your mouth dear, before you catch flies. Don't worry dear, I'm not leaving you. I'm happy with our marriage and I'm happy with you, but I want to fuck another man tonight. Don't wait up and don't forget to sleep in one of the spare bedrooms."

She turned and walked out of the room, down the stairs and out into the attached garage and minutes later, her BMW went down the drive while I stood stunned in the bedroom.

Even though she had told me not to wait up I was up when she came home. How the hell did she expect me to be able to sleep after the bomb she laid on me? I heard the garage door opener start to run and I looked out the window to see her BMW coming up the drive followed by another car. I was standing in the kitchen when Ada came through the connecting door from the garage. She saw me standing there and shrugged her shoulders, "It would have been better for you, ego wise, had you been in the spare bedroom just now, but if you want it this way so be it." She started for the front door and then she stopped and turned to me.

"Your position in this house and in this marriage is safe as long as you don't do anything stupid. When I let Dave in I will introduce you and you will smile and shake his hand and then you can come up and watch for all I care. If you can't handle this, or if you make a scene, you can pack your bags and get out and my lawyers will be in touch, understand?"

I just stood there, not understanding what was happening and she said with a touch of steel in her voice, "I said do you understand?"

I numbly shook my head yes.

"Good. Now either get ready to meet Dave or run along up to a spare bedroom."

I don't know why I tagged along behind her; I suppose it was because I didn't really believe it was happening, maybe it was some sort of joke or some kind of test or something. I was standing three feet from Ada when she opened the door and let the man in. I was surprised to see that he was black.

"Dave, this is my husband Jerry. Jerry, this is Dave and he will be taking your place in our bed tonight."

Dave gave me a goofy grin and stuck out his hand and I numbly took it and shook it.

"As long as you are up dear, would you make us a couple of drinks and bring them up to the bedroom please? I'll have my usual and Dave drinks scotch on the rocks, Dewars if we have it. Come along Dave and I'll show you the playroom" and the two of them walked away and left me standing there.

I was seething. I wanted to break something. I wanted to smash Dave in the mouth. I wanted to take a belt and beat Ada's ass bloody. Those are the things I wanted to do, but what I did was make the drinks, put them on a tray and carry them upstairs. Dave was sitting on the edge of the bed with his trousers down around his ankles and Ada was kneeling in front of him sucking his worthless black cock. When I walked into the room Ada took her mouth off of him long enough to say, "Set the drinks on the bedside stand and then run along dear. I'll see you in the morning."

I'd been dismissed and had been told to get out.

<<O>>

I had a lot on my mind as I walked away from what was supposed to be my bedroom to one of the spare bedrooms. Chief among my thoughts was what was I going to do about my new situation. I knew the answer to that before the question was fully formed. Nothing. I would do nothing. I would do absolutely nothing except smile and bear it. Ada controlled the purse strings and she kept a very tight grip on them. I couldn't complain because Ada denied me nothing. If I wanted it, I got it. I wanted a house with grounds, a swimming pool and a tennis court so Ada went out, found it and bought it. I wanted a Corvette so

Ada went out and bought me one. Country club membership? No problem. A week in Aspen? Mention it and the tickets would be on the desk in my den when I got home from work and the reservations at the lodge would be already made. I lacked for nothing. Ada showered me with jewelry, clothes, sports gear and she even saw to it that the balance in my checking account never fell below five grand. And that didn't even count my own paycheck. I actually tried to give it Ada to add to the 'household account' but she wouldn't take it.

"Put it in savings Jerry, or invest it. You made it, you keep it."

She spoiled me rotten, but she wasn't stupid. I had to sign a prenuptial agreement before we got married. If I divorced her I got nothing. If she divorced me before the marriage was ten years in existence I got a lump sum settlement of one hundred grand. After ten years, I got an additional twenty grand for each year exceeding ten. No, Ada could rub my face in an awful lot and I'd still smile and take it. I didn't understand it, but I would take it.

The reason I didn't understand it was because Ada and I had what I considered to be a pretty damned good sex life. Every night of the week was not uncommon, although the actual average was probably only five nights a week and we did it all. She liked to be eaten and I liked eating her. She gave fantastic head and loved anal sex. In addition, I really did love Ada. I know that it was her money that caused me to go after her, but I was very fond of her by our wedding and it grew into love. What had gone wrong? I probably should have picked a room farther away from what used to be my bedroom, because all I heard for the next several hours were the yells, moans, and cries that Ada used to make with me. I finally fell asleep, but it was a very fitful sleep. I woke up when I heard a car door slam and I got up and looked out the window and saw Dave's car backing out of the drive. I looked over at the clock and saw that it was four in the morning. I debated going back to my bedroom to try and talk to Ada, but then I said, "Fuck it!" and went back to bed.

<<O>>

The morning brought another surprise. I don't know what I expected when I woke up, but it certainly wasn't what I expected. Ada was climbing into bed with me and going down on me as though the previous night hadn't happened. When she got me hard, she climbed on top and slid down my pole and I felt Dave. She hadn't cleaned herself before coming to me and I wondered if it was another way of rubbing my nose in her infidelity. As if reading my mind, she said, "Can you feel him Jerry? Can you feel what Dave left in me? Do you like the feeling of soaking your cock in a black man's juices? He fucked me five times Jerry, five marvelous times. But you know what Jerry? As good as he was, you are still my man. You are going to be sharing me a lot from now on, but you are still my man." She rolled off me and pulled at me, "Come on Jerry, climb in the saddle and fuck me. Do me hard baby, do me hard."

I didn't say a word to Ada. I fucked her, finished, got out of bed and took a shower to wash the cum and sweat off me and then I did my daily twenty-five laps in the pool. That done, I went into the house and put on the coffee pot and I was sitting at the table drinking coffee and reading the morning paper when Ada came into the kitchen. I ignored her and after several minutes of silence, she said, "You are a grown man Jerry. It doesn't suit you to act like an upset little kid."

"Upset doesn't cover it Ada. I don't have anything to say right now. I'm keeping my mouth shut until you see fit to explain what game it is that you are playing."

"No game Jerry, I've just decided that I want to fuck other men from now on. You don't have to put up with it if you don't want to. Just pack and leave, but I meant what I said, you are still my main man if you want to be. You just have to get used to sharing me."

"That's it? Get used to sharing you or get out?"

"That's it in a nutshell Jerry."

Share her I did, but I never got used to it. Over the course of the next six months, on an average of twice a week Ada would tell me to sleep in a spare bedroom while she entertained in our bedroom. I never understood why, but the men she always brought home were black. The first couple of times I made sure that I was in the spare bedroom when she got home with her stud of the evening. The next morning she would crawl in bed with me and describe her evening as she slid up and down on my dick and when she had finished telling me all about it, she would roll over and pull me on top of her and tell me to fuck her hard.

Then I guess she decided that she wasn't rubbing my nose in her infidelities hard enough. She started telling me to wait up for her, that she wanted me to meet her lovers and from there it went to having me wait on them, bring them drinks and snacks and in one case she even sent one of them to me to ask if he could borrow one of my condoms. I half expected Ada to tell me to roll it on him, but I was spared that indignity. A dozen times I almost told Ada to kiss my ass, but then I would look out the window at the swimming pool and the tennis courts and I would think of all the material things that Ada provided and I would get my anger in check and just go on being the good cuckolded husband.

I got the glass of water and carried it back into the bedroom and as I handed it to the smirking black asshole, something inside me just snapped. It was like a switch had been thrown and all of a sudden everything was different - totally different. I'd like to say that I stuffed the glass down the black asshole's throat, but I didn't. I handed it to him and he said, "Thank you" and I said, "You're welcome" and I left the room.

I wasn't in the spare bedroom in the morning. In fact, I wasn't even in the house. I came home at five in the afternoon to a very angry Ada.

"Where in the hell have you been?"

"Out taking care of business."

"What kind of business?"

"Well, let's just see what we have in here" and I opened my briefcase. I took out some papers and started handing them to her. "Here is the check for the last five thousand that you put in my checking account. Do you know that they got upset when I closed the account? They actually asked me if you were aware that I was doing it. Here is the title to the Corvette. I've signed off on the back of it. Maybe you can give it to last night's lover. He looks like the kind of guy who could be happy in a Vette."

I rummaged around in my briefcase, "Let's see what else I have in here. Oh here, these are for you" and I took out a key ring. One by one I took them off the ring and laid them down on the table as I said,

"The key to the house, the keys to the Vette, this one is to my locker at the country club. The clubs you gave me for my birthday are inside of it and I'm sure that one of your lovers would like to have them. Last, but by all means least, as you have shown me over the last six months, is this." I slid my wedding ring off my finger and tossed it on the table. There was a honking from out front and I said, "My cab is here. I'll drop you a line when I find a place to stay so you will know where to send the papers."

I got up and headed for the door as Ada screamed at me, "Jerry, you get back here. You get back here right this minute."

I ignored her and then I was out the front door and gone.

It was halfway through the third round when the right staggered me and I went to my knees. I was up by the seven count, which, on reflection, was a very bad move on my part. I was still seeing double when he moved in on me and I never saw the punch that knocked me out. I came to in the dressing room and I thought I heard a familiar voice ask, "Will he be all right?"

"He should be fine. Some double vision for a while and maybe a little nausea, but no other harmful effects."

"Thank God. I was afraid of the way he went down that he was hurt really bad."

A chuckle and then, "It's the price he pays for the fun he has."

"When can I take him home?"

"I thought he lived alone?"

"Not anymore, not if I can help it."

It slowly got through to me that the voice was Ada's. What was she doing here? I'd put her out of my life six months ago. The whiff of the smelling salts being passed under my nose almost brought me up to a sitting position and I looked around the room and saw Doc Jeffers and Ada.

"You really ought to give this up Jerry" Doc said, "You are just a bit past your prime."

"Got to pay the rent Doc."

"Whatever. I'll be going now. No fights for two weeks and I

really wish you wouldn't have any more at all."

As the door closed him I looked at Ada and said, "What are you doing here?"

"I've come to take you home."

"How you going to do that? You don't even know where I live."

"Of course I do. I sit out in front of the place every night trying to work up the courage to walk up and ring your doorbell."

"What? It takes more guts to ring a doorbell than to drag men in front of me and then fuck them?"

She looked away from me and in a timid voice said, "Yes, yes it does."

"Why do you want to ring my doorbell in the first place?"

"So I can talk to you. So I can try and get you to come back home."

"That whorehouse (and I put a lot of emphasis on 'whorehouse') is not my home."

"Then we'll sell it and buy another."

"Go away Ada. I put you out of my life. It's been six months now and I've managed to get along just fine."

"I haven't."

"You haven't what?"

"Managed to get along just fine. I haven't slept well since you left. I'm having trouble eating and my nerves are a mess."

"Sex is supposed to help all those things and you were dragging plenty of that home with you as I recall."

"There hasn't been a man in my life since the day you left."

I'm sure that my facial expression said, "Yeah, right!"

"I mean it Jerry. There hasn't been a man in my life since that day you walked out on me and you were the only man in my life when you were there."

I laughed out loud when I heard that one and she said, "No Jerry, seriously. You were the only man in my life, the others were just tools."

"Tools?"

"Yes. All they were were things I used because I was stupid."

"You lost me there."

"I got to thinking that you didn't love me and that you only married me for my money. I thought about it so much that I convinced myself that I needed to find out. So I decided to do something that would show me one way or the other. I decided that I had to do something so that you would have to do something about it if you loved me. If you didn't love me and were only with me for my money you would just turn your back on it and let me get away with it rather than risk a fight that would end our relationship. You were supposed to throw Dave out on his ass that first time, either that or grab your clothes and leave, but you were not supposed to let me get away with it. When you let me take Dave to our bedroom it broke my heart. When you let him fuck me and you were still there the next day, I knew that you didn't love me, only my money.

"After Dave the others were just my way of showing you how disgusted I was with you and I even made sure that all of them were black to piss you off more. Then you left me and I found out something that I hadn't realized. I found out that it didn't matter if you didn't love me and only wanted me for my money, for what I had. I found out that I loved you and couldn't live without you. Since you walked out, I've been a mess. I spend all my time following you around. I've been here for every one of your fights sitting in the back where you couldn't see me.

"I sit outside your apartment. I even rented an office across the street from yours and from my office window I can look down into yours and I sit there and watch you all day long. I can't live without you Jerry. I don't care if you don't really love me, I need you Jerry, I need you."

I'm not totally stupid and even though it wasn't true, I knew what to say:

"I didn't stay through all of that shit for your money Ada. I stayed because I loved you and I hoped that whatever it was that you were doing would work its way out of your system. I finally couldn't take it anymore. It was obvious that you didn't love me or you couldn't have done to me what you did so I did the only thing I could do and I left and I don't see any reason for me to even be talking to you now. You made your bed Ada, go lie in it and leave me alone."

"Please Jerry, please. We can work it out, I know we can. Please Jerry, please come home with me."

There was no question that I was going to let myself be persuaded, but I wanted to be a little mean and do some nose rubbing of my own. If she didn't go for it, I could back off, but I wanted to see just how desperate she was to have me back.

"You hurt me Ada. You have no idea what it did to me to be put through what you put me through. I can't see getting back together with you without giving you a taste of what you did to me. Who is your best girlfriend?"

"I suppose that it would be Linda Meyer."

"Is she the sexy looking redhead whose husband is the dentist?"

"Yes."

"Okay Ada, here's the deal. I want you to bring Linda into our bedroom just the way you brought all those men. Then I want you to stand there and watch me fuck Linda just like I had to stand there and watch you fuck all those black assholes. I want you to serve Linda and me snacks and drinks just like you had me do. I'm not going to fuck as many women as you did men, but I am going to do the one."

"I can't do that! She's happily married and has three kids."

"I don't give a shit Ada. You want me and I want revenge. Make it happen or get used to me not being around. Until then, just leave me alone."

<<O>>

That was two weeks ago and I honestly didn't expect that it would happen, but I wanted to make Ada sweat and suffer a little. I expected her to come back in a week or two and tell me that it just couldn't be done and then do some more begging and pleading.

Ada just called me:

"You can come home tonight Jerry. Linda will be here at seven, but there is a slight complication." She would only agree to do it if would agree to spend a night with her husband next week."

"So what's the problem?"

"I'm your wife Jerry. I'm trying to put us back together again. How can I do that if I'm having sex with another man?"

"Ada, you were a cock sucking whore for six months, so just what is one more cock to you?"

There was silence on the other end of the line and then, "Tell me to do it Jerry. If you tell me to do it, I won't be cheating on you."

"How can you cheat on me when we aren't even together Ada? I told you what you had to do to get me to even consider coming back to you. You make up your mind Ada and then you let me know" and I hung up on her.

She called me back in ten minutes, "All right Jerry, I'll fuck him, just come home tonight baby, please just come home."

"Look on the bright side Ada, at least you'll be fucking a white man for a change" and I burst out laughing as I hung up the phone.

End of the 2nd Story

Amy's Security

I had slipped in unnoticed, gotten a drink from the bar and then I had moved to a dark corner where I could unobtrusively watch the goings on. The lateness of the hour and the cleared tables suggested that the dinner part of the festivities was over and more than likely so was all the speechifying and the dispensing of bonuses. Now it was more of a cocktail party. The tables had been moved back to create a dance floor and a five-piece band was setting up. My attention was centered on the reason I had come to the affair. I watched as she moved through the crowd talking to the people and looking for all the world like she was the hostess.

<<O>>

I sensed him before he spoke, "She sure is something, isn't she."

I turned and saw a short, ruddy-faced man standing to my left and slightly behind me. He stuck out his hand, "Jack Branscomb. I work out of the Omaha office."

I took his hand and introduced myself and said, "You know her?"

"Not near as well as I would like. I came close once, but close only counts in horseshoes and hand grenades, right?"

I was intrigued by his statement, "You came close? How was that?"

"You new to the company? You don't know who she is?"

"I'm just a guest."

"Well, little Amy there is the boss' private stock, but when the mood strikes him he will share. The Omaha branch has been the poorest producing branch in the company. One day the boss and Amy flew into town. The boss had all the sales people come into the office for a meeting and then he read us the riot act. Turn the place around or he would shut the office down and we could all go looking for new jobs. And then he said:

"But to give you a little incentive I'll make it interesting and throw in a prize for the highest producer. Amy, show the boys what the winner will get."

"Amy did a strip for the boys that would have put a professional stripper to shame and then the boss said, "One night with Amy to the highest scoring salesman." I missed by a lousy two grand. My sales were a million, five hundred and sixty-two thousand, but Miller beat me by eighteen hundred dollars. Miller, that's him over there, said that Amy showed him what heaven would be like. Hey, there goes my regional manager, got to go and suck up" and he left me standing there staring at my wife and wondering if I knew her at all.

It was Amy's company Christmas party and I wasn't supposed to be there. I was supposed to be in New York on business, but things moved a lot faster than expected and I was able to fly home two days earlier than planned. I tried reaching Amy to let her know, but her office had closed for the day and all I got at home was the answering machine. When the plane landed I saw that there was still enough time to hit the party, have a couple of drinks and then take Amy home and try to make up for a week of going without. Now I didn't know if I should even bother going home at all.

The idea that my wife was the company whore was ludicrous at first glance, but Jack had not equivocated at all when he made his statements. Amy was the Executive Secretary to Jason Billings, the president and CEO of the company and she did travel with him when he visited the outlying offices. And she had made three trips to Omaha that year. My heart was crying out "Bullshit!" but my gut was saying "Check it out."

I stayed in my corner and nursed my drink and watched Miller. After half an hour he did what I was waiting for. He put his drink down and headed for the bathrooms and I set my glass down and followed him. Luckily he was the only one in the bathroom when I walked in. I stepped up to the urinal next to the one he was whizzing in and I looked over at him, "Miller, right?"

He nodded and said; "Do I know you?"

"Nope, never met, but you are my hero."

He gave me a funny look like he thought maybe I was trying to hit on him and then said, "Why am I your hero?"

"Because you scored Amy Beckman. Do you know how many guys in the company would cut off their left hand just to have coffee with her? You got to spend a whole night with her. I got to tell you that that puts you pretty high on the list of people I'd like to be like."

I saw the relief on his face when he realized I wasn't a fag trying to pick him up and he smiled.

"Just the luck of the draw. Jack Branscomb was ten thousand ahead of me going into the last day of the contest. I told all my customers about the contest and the prize and almost all of them kicked their orders up a grand or two and that gave me just enough to ace out Jack. Hey, if you ever get a shot you had best lie, cheat, steal or do whatever you have to do because she is totally worth it."

He started digging for his wallet and when he got it out and open he took out a Polaroid snapshot and showed it to me. "I keep this to inspire me on days when sales are slow."

It was Amy all right, in all of her naked glory. "Oh man," I said wistfully, "Some guys have all the luck." Yeah, and some guys get it broken off in their ass, especially trusting husbands.

I went back to my dark corner and settled in to watch. Amy didn't expect to see me for two more days and I was curious to see what would happen. When the party started breaking up, I moved out to the hotel lobby and sat down where I could watch the doors to the ballroom. Jason and Amy were the last to leave and I had a paper that I was pretending to read in front of my face when they walked by me. I heard Jason say, "….. leave yours here and come back for it in the morning?"

"No, you can follow….." and then they were out of earshot. I guessed that Jason was going to follow Amy to our house and I needed to beat them there so I could erase the answering machine tape.

I drove like a mad man and broke every speed limit in town. Any light that caught me I ran and all a stop sign was to me was something to look at as I blew by. I parked around the corner and ran to the house, let myself in and dashed for the answering machine. I hit PLAY and as soon as my message started, I hit the DELETE button and then I hurried to the hall closet where I kept the camera bag. I took out the Nikon and checked to see what I had left on the roll and then I took the camera bag and ran up the stairs. I set the video camera up where it wouldn't be noticed and then I focused it in on the bed. At the last minute I remembered the little red light and I ran to the bathroom and got a Band-Aid to cover it.

Five minutes later I heard the garage door opener start to run and I left the bedroom and moved to the head of the stairs and peeked around the corner. Amy came in and headed straight for the wet bar and fixed a couple of drinks and about two minutes later Jason let himself in the front door. The bastard had a key to my house!

Amy walked over to him and handed him a drink and tilted her face up for a kiss. Jason took the drink and then bent and gave Amy a kiss on the lips that seemed to have a little tongue action with it and then the two of them went over and sat down on the couch.

"I think everything went well tonight. You did a great job as usual."

Amy grinned, "That's why you pay me the big bucks."

"No it isn't and you know it. I pay you the big bucks because you are the hottest piece of ass this side of the Mississippi. Your efficiency in other areas is just an unexpected bonus. Speaking of which, I hope you were happy with the size of yours?"

"You were more than generous Jason."

"It should have been more, especially since you wrapped Feldman around your little finger last night. He couldn't say enough good things about you. Did he stay the night?"

"Yes, and I got damned little rest out of it. He is especially fond of anal and my pooper is still a little sore. You will have to settle for blow jobs and pussy tonight."

"I thought you would never ask" and he stood up and undressed.

Amy downed her drink and then got on her knees in front of him. "All the way?"

"Yeah baby, I want to cum in your mouth to start out the night."

"How long can you stay?"

"All night baby. Nancy is staying with her sister for three days. How long before I have to be out?"

"You can stay until tomorrow night. Hubby flies in at two the next day."

"Why can't I stay over night tomorrow too?"

"Because I want to be fresh as a Daisy when Mark gets home

and that big cock of yours stretches me. I have to give it time to shrink a little."

"You sure that he doesn't expect anything?"

"Nope sweetie, he is clueless. He loves me and as far as he is concerned, I can do no wrong."

And then she lowered her head and started sucking Jason's cock. Jason leaned back on the couch and I saw a satisfied smile come over his face. I wanted to go down there and smash his face in, but I held my anger in check. I'd get my revenge, but it would be my way. I'd had several friends who had gone through divorces and they had been raped and left bleeding by the courts and the lawyers and I was determined that it wasn't going to happen to me. But I needed the right pictures and I needed Amy to get Jason up to the bedroom where the video camera could tape them. Pictures with sound are so much better than stills, but I still needed the Nikon for back up.

Down on the couch, I saw Jason archs his hips up off the couch, and I could see Amy's throat moving as she swallowed his load.

"God baby, but you are the absolute greatest at that," he said as Amy stood up and started stripping. When she was down to just nylons and high heels, she did a slow turn in front of him.

"You like?"

"You know I do, baby. I can't get enough of you."

"That's good lover because Amy is horny tonight, so let's get upstairs and see what you can do to help me resolve my problem."

Jason got up off the couch and with Amy leading the way he headed for the stairway. I moved back to the bedroom and got in the closet and moments later the two of them entered the room. Amy went right to the bed and spread herself for Jason.

"Eat me sweetie," she said as he got on the bed with her. He dutifully lowered his head and Amy moaned as his tongue and lips went to work on her. Amy still had her heels and hose on and I don't believe that I had ever seen a more erotic sight than Amy, legs spread wide and her black CFMs digging in as she pushed her cunt up at Jason's mouth. Erotic, but not what I was looking for in the way of photos.

After several minutes Amy moaned, "Are you hard yet lover?"

Jason took his mouth off her long enough to say, "As a rock sweetie" and he went back to muff diving.

"I want it Jason. I want your cock. I'm ready lover, fuck me, fuck my brains out."

Jason moved up and Amy reached down and used a hand to guide him into her cunt, "Oh god sweetie, that feels good, that feels so god damned good. I love your big cock in me Jason. Fuck me sweetie, fuck me."

Jason drove his cock in her and started pounding away and Amy was crying out, "Fuck me, fuck me, harder Jason, harder."

I was on edge. I wanted to burst out of the closet and start taking pictures with the Nikon, but I wanted as much video as I could get. I most especially wanted the portions where Amy was screaming out Jason's name. I had to force myself to stand there and watch and listen.

The most surprising thing about the situation, at least to me, was that as I watched and listened, I was sporting the stiffest hard on I'd had in years. And then Jason started getting vocal.

"Who's your daddy?"

"You are baby, you are."

"Whose cock owns you?"

"Yours Jason, your cock owns me. I live for your cock baby, I crave it."

"Is your daddy better than your husband?"

"Much better baby, much better. Make me cum daddy, make me cum."

"Who has the bigger cock baby?"

"You do daddy, I love your big cock. Fuck me baby, fuck me hard."

I'd heard and seen enough and I pushed open the closet door and moved towards the bed. I got five good exposures before the two of them realized that they weren't alone. Suddenly Amy was screaming and struggling to get out from under Jason and Jason was scrambling to get away from Amy and off the bed. I just kept moving around and taking pictures until I ran out of film. Jason ran out of the bedroom and down the stairs to where his clothes were and a minute or two later I heard the front door slam.

On the bed Amy was crying and trying to talk at the same time. "What are you doing here," she said, more as an accusation than as a question, "You're supposed to be in New York."

"Yeah. Well Amy, I guess you just can't depend on me for nothing."

"What are you going to do?"

"I'll check into a motel tonight and see a lawyer first thing in the morning. After that I'll step back and take a look at what's left."

"Why are you going to see a lawyer?"

"Because that seems to be the way that you go about getting a divorce."

"Divorce?"

"Yeah sweetie, that is what usually happens when one partner in a marriage catches the other being unfaithful and from what I've learned tonight you have been unfaithful in bunches. I'll have the lawyer arrange for a time when I can come back and pick up my stuff. Preferably with you not here."

I turned to leave and she cried out, "Don't go Sam, I can explain. It isn't what you think" and I just kept on walking.

<<O>>

I was not surprised when I went into work the next morning to find seven messages for Amy on my voice mail. I deleted them and got to work. About nine, my secretary stuck her head in my office, "I have your wife on line three."

I was all set to tell her to disconnect and to not take any more calls from Amy, but then I thought that it would be unfair to Megan to put her in the middle. I lifted the handset and pressed the button for line three.

"Yes?"

"Come home Sam. I cried all night. I love you honey and I need you here."

"Tough shit Amy. I don't want to be anywhere near you."

"Can we at least get together and sit down and talk?"

"I don't see any need Amy. I heard enough last night just listening to you and Jason. I can't for the life of me think of what you could have to say that would make what I heard irrelevant."

"I don't know what you heard Sam, but I can explain if you will just give me a chance."

"Okay Amy, where and when?"

"I don't want to do it in public Sam. Just come home tonight and we can talk."

"I'll go along Amy, but you need to know that I know a whole lot more than you might think. The first time I catch you in a lie or even shading the truth a little, I'm gone."

"Fair enough. I'll be there by six."

I arrived at six-ten and found Amy sitting at the kitchen table, an open bottle of white wine in front of her and two filled glasses on the table.

"Getting me drunk isn't going to help Amy."

"I know, but maybe the wine will loosen a little of the tension."

"There is no tension on my side of the table Amy, just a regret that something that I thought was so good was really rotten to the core."

"Please Sam, give me a chance to explain. It isn't what you think."

"Let me tell you what I think Amy – no, make that let me tell you what I know. I know you are a whore. I know of three men who you have fucked this year and from what I've been hearing the number is probably considerably more. I saw you fucking Jason; I heard you tell him how much Feldman liked fucking your asshole and a man named Miller was all too happy to show me a naked picture of you and tell me what a marvelous night he spent with you. A contest prize for God's sake. You were a contest prize for some fucking geek from Omaha. What can you possibly say to make those things go away?"

"Okay Sam, I get the picture. I'm a whore, a round-heeled slut, the company punchboard, but there is a reason for it all and that's what I want to explain. It won't make it go away and it won't heal wounds, but I need for you to know why I did what I did, even if you won't accept it or understand it."

"All right, go ahead, I'm listening."

"I'm ambitious Sam. I want more out of my life, at least job wise. I busted my ass to get to be Jason's secretary so I could use it as a springboard and it was working, at least until last night. I haven't seen or spoken to Jason since he left the house last night so I don't know what my status is right now. Jerry Winters is retiring next month and Jason was going to give me Jerry's position. I'd be Vice President of Sales and the odds on favorite to take over as president and CEO when Jason decides to hang it up.

"So I did a few things that were outside the bounds of our marriage, but so what? I wouldn't be the first woman who slept her way to the top. Besides, it isn't like it cost you anything – you were never home. Are your skirts clean Sam? You never got a taste of strange while you were out there on the road doing business for your company?"

"Yes Amy, my skirts are clean. I had chances, lots of them. Women who were dangled in front of me like you were dangled in front of Feldman, but I always said no Amy. I always said no because I knew I had something better waiting at home for me. But I guess that I really didn't, did I?"

"Of course you did. I love you Sam, you know that. You have to know that. We couldn't have been together as long as we have without you knowing it. What I did while you were gone didn't change the way I feel about you."

"It sure didn't sound like it last night. I distinctly heard you shooting me through the grease while you and Jason were bouncing around on the bed."

"Honey, that was all bullshit. While you were taking pictures did you happen to notice the size of Jason's weenie? It is half the size of yours. Like most men who feel they are inferior on some level Jason needs his ego stroked. That's all it was honey, just bullshit to make Jason feel better about himself. Nothing more Sam, I swear."

"It doesn't change anything Amy. You are still a cheating wife and a whore. What is so god damned important about you being a VP or getting to be president and CEO. I make more than enough for the two of us. You never had to go to work in the first place."

"That's where you are wrong Sam. I need the security that climbing the corporate ladder will give me."

"So now, on top of everything else, you are saying that I'm not a good provider."

"Oh, you're a great provider Sam, now, but what about next year or the year after that? You are a heart attack Sam, just looking for a time and place to happen. Your job and the way you do it are going to kill you Sam. You are on the road three weeks out of five, eating bad food and sitting in lounges and drinking in the evenings because you have nothing better to do. When you come home, you spend ten or twelve hours a day at the office and still bring work home to do in the evenings and on the weekends.

"When you go Sam, and I'm standing there looking down into the casket all I'm going to have are memories, equity in the house and a half million dollars in life insurance. Half a million sounds like a lot, but it isn't. If I try to keep the house I'd have to use a lot of it to pay the mortgage off or at least down far enough that I could refinance and get a payment that I could afford to make. Taxes being what they are would take some of it and then I would have to pay off all of our debts because I couldn't make the payments on an executive secretary's pay. I wouldn't have much left and I'd still have to work to get by."

"Well, you are right about one thing Amy, you are certainly going to need the security because we are through. There might have been a chance – a real small one – that we might have survived your having an affair. I could maybe understand and forgive that. But I can't accept what you have been doing, no way."

"If you try to divorce me Sam, I'll fight you every step of the way. I'll get the best divorce lawyer around and I'll fight it. I love you and I know that you love me and I know that we can work through this."

"You won't fight me Amy. You know why? Because of your precious security, that's why. Right now you can go to Jason and say, "I'm free lover, we don't have to sneak around behind Sam's back any more. Who do you want me to fuck next?" But if you fight me, I'll drag you and Jason through the mud. I'll see to it that his wife gets copies of all the photos and when she's done with Jason you'll be lucky to have a job at all, let alone a position as a vice president. It is your choice Amy and if I were you I would think long and hard on it. Now, as long as I'm here, I'm going to go upstairs and pack a few things."

I grabbed a bag and tossed some shirts and underwear in it and then I got the video camera from where I'd hidden it and tossed it into the bag. Then I headed back downstairs. Amy was standing at the bottom of the stairs with tears running down her cheeks.

"Please Sam, please don't do this. I love you Sam, honest to god I do. We can work things out honey, just give it a chance."

I shook my head and said, "Goodbye Amy" and walked out.

The next morning I showed up at Jason's office bright and early; so early that he wasn't even there yet. I was sitting in a chair just outside his office door when he got there. His face turned pale and his step faltered when he saw me, but he put on a show of bravado, "You are the last person that I would have expected to see here."

"I came to make you an offer that you can't refuse."

When I left his office, I had secured Amy's security for her. She would get the Vice President of Sales position and all I had to do was promise that the photos I took would never be seen by Jason's wife. I told him that he had that promise as long as he treated Amy fairly.

"Treat her right and you will never hear from me again. Fuck over her and not only your wife, but everybody else will see them."

"Why are you doing this for her? I would have thought that under the circumstances, you would have gone after her like Attila the Hun scouring the Steppes of Russia."

"Once upon a time I loved her and she loved me. That has to be worth something."

"She still loves you. What she did has nothing to do with how she feels about you."

"Maybe not, but it does to me."

The divorce was final two years ago. I get cards from Amy on Christmas, Easter, Valentines Day, Sweetest Day, my birthday and any other holiday she can get a card for and they are always signed, "Much love, Amy" and all with the PS "Please call me some time, I miss you." So far I haven't. She got her VP slot and since then has been promoted to Executive Vice President in Charge of Operations.

In a case of supreme irony, Jason's company bought out my company and I am presently working in the department headed by my ex-wife. Everyone in my old company knows that there will be reorganization in the near future and that a lot of positions will be eliminated because of duplication. I have no idea of where I am sitting on the totem pole, but won't it be a major kick in the ass if my seeing to Amy's security costs me mine?

End of the 3ʳᵈ Story

Adele's Problem

I looked down at the pile on the table in front of me and wondered just where the habit had come from and how I'd gotten started doing it. I always peel the labels off of my beer bottles. I had been sitting there for over an hour and a half waiting for my stepmother to show and the pile had grown. Adele had called me at work and had asked me to meet her for a drink. She said that she had something important that she needed to talk to me about and so far she had called me twice on her cell to tell me that she was running late, but that she was on the way.

Normally I won't sit around and wait for people who are late for meetings and appointments, but this time curiosity had me pinned to my chair. Adele and I did not get along - never had - and I didn't expect that we ever would. I did have to admit that I was as much to blame for the animosity as she was. After mom had died, I thought dad had replaced her way too soon and so I was a little cold toward Adele when she moved in. On her part Adele was way too bossy for someone new to the household and to the two teenagers who lived there.

For some reason my sister Vickie had warmed to Adele right away, but Adele hadn't been there three days before she was telling me what to do and how to do it. That is something that you just don't do to a naturally rebellious teenager who is still grieving over the loss of his mother. And it had never gotten any better.

I went to college on a football scholarship and I had hardly ever gone back home. Spring Break, the holidays, summer vacation were all spent some place else and if my dad wanted to see me he had to come and visit me because I wouldn't go home if Adele was there. He would visit and try to mend fences, "It was just as hard for Adele to come into that situation as it was for you to have her there. She means well, and she tries hard. Try and meet her halfway." He never did understand that there were two problems - Adele, and the fact that I had never forgiven him for his obscene (to me anyway) quickness in replacing mom.

I graduated, got a job, met a girl and got married and, more to please Sandra than for any other reason, I made an effort to maintain family ties with dad and Adele. It wasn't all that hard since I didn't live with them anymore, but Adele and I never managed to get past an armed truce. And now, out of the blue, she wanted to meet me for a drink.

I saw her come in the front door of the bar and I noticed every male head in the place turn to look at her and appreciate her beauty. I didn't like her much, but I am not blind. Looking at her it was easy to see why my father had gone after her. Even at forty-three she had the nice tight look of a girl twenty years younger. She keeps that look with daily sessions on the Stairmaster down in the basement and with five mile runs three days a week. In spite of myself, I felt my cock twitch as she walked toward the table. I stood up as she reached my table and she offered me her hand.

"Thank you for agreeing to meet me here and I'm sorry to be so late. There was something that I needed to get done before meeting you and the person I had to see was himself late."

She sat down and I asked her what she was drinking and she said, "Scotch on the rocks, Dewar's if they have it." I got up to get it and when I got back to the table she was taking a large envelope out of her purse and setting it on the table. She took a sip of her drink, set the glass down and cut right to the chase.

"I have a major problem and I'm trying to figure out what to do about it. Frankly, I did not realize that it was also your problem until yesterday."

"My problem too?"

"Yes. Before I go into it, I need to clear the decks so to speak. First off I know you don't like me and it may surprise you to know that I completely understand it, but your father was the best thing to ever happen to me and I wasn't going to let him get away. I was not going to wait around a year or two and take the chance that he might find someone else. I am not now, nor will I ever apologize for that. Next, you need to understand that I love your father wholly and completely and regardless of what happens I have no intention of losing him to someone else or of tossing his worthless ass out on the street."

Adele saw the look that came over my face and said, "Yes, I just said in the same sentence that I love your father and that he is worthless. That brings me to our problem. Your father is having an affair."

"How is my father having an affair my problem?"

"He is having the affair with Sandra."

"What? You must be joking."

"I wish I was."

She slid the brown envelope over to me. "The reason I am so late is that I had to meet the private detective I hired so I could pick up these. They are really quite explicit. He had to bribe quite a few people to get the cameras in place to get these images."

I opened the envelope and took out several eight by ten prints. Adele was right - they were very explicit. Sandra on her knees with a cock in her mouth, Sandra on her knees with a cock in her ass and Sandra in fourteen other positions with a cock in one hole or another and in each case the cock was attached to my father. I was stunned. Sandra is cheating on me! Why? When?

"How long has this been going on?"

"I don't know. I only became aware that he was up to something three weeks ago when I found a condom in his pocket while doing the laundry. He doesn't need them with me because I had a hysterectomy six years ago. I didn't say anything to him at the time, but it ate away at me and so I hired a detective to find out what was going on. I didn't know he was seeing Sandra until I got the detective's report last night. He followed Sandra home from the hotel and when he gave me her name and address it was the first I knew that it was your wife."

She watched my face for several seconds and then said, "You had no idea? She gave you no reason to suspect anything?"

I shook my head, "None. I'm not even aware of there being a problem between us that would cause her to have an affair with anyone, let alone dad."

"Yes, well, he is, or rather, they are. The reason I asked you to meet me here was so we can discuss what will happen next."

"What do you mean?"

"Well, before yesterday when I found out that my problem was also your problem, I had already decided on a course of action. I did not intend to let your father know directly that I knew. Instead, I was going to repay him in kind and let him find out. Then I was going to fuck up his extracurricular love life in a way that would make him feel guilty as hell. That is, that is what I was going to do until I found out that it was

Sandra."

"What were you going to do?"

"Take on several lovers, get them to leave a few love bites in strategic places, wait until your father noticed them and said something and then drop the photos on him. Then I was going to find a way to set up the bimbo he was fucking and get her thrown in jail for a year or so. Your father would know I did it and why and he would have felt guilty as hell for causing it to happen and he would have made certain that it never happened again. I can't do that now, at least not the second part anyway."

"Why not?"

"Because dummy, it would affect you and even though you hate my guts you are still family and I don't fuck over family - unless of course they fuck over me first. So the question now is, what do we do?"

She was a fucking animal in bed. She screamed and hollered, begged and pleaded. Her heels drummed on the backs of my legs so hard that I suspected that they would be bruised when we left the hotel. She spread the photos out on the floor and we re-enacted each and every one.

If Sandra took it in the ass, so did Adele; Sandra sucked cock and so did Adele. She was insatiable and as fast as I came and lost my hard on Adele went to work to get me another one. Finally, I was beat. I just could not get it up again no matter how hard Adele tried.

The plan had been to split the pictures, take a room, make love, mark each other and then go home. When our spouses commented on the love bites we would drop the photos on them and say, "If it is good enough for you, it's good enough for me" and then go from there. But about an hour into things when I went to give Adele a hickey on her breast she cried out, "No, no, don't, not yet, not yet." I wondered why she was departing from the plan. I can be a little on the dense side sometimes, but it was not until I was plowing her tight asshole that I realized that if we marked each other it would be over as soon as the marks were noticed. Unmarked we could do it again, and again and again. After we had dressed Adele gathered up the photos and put them back in her purse.

"We don't need to split them just yet, do we? At least not for a little while?"

"Maybe not ever" I said as I took her in my arms and kissed her, "Maybe not ever."

End of the 4ᵗʰ Story

Marybeth Strikes

My sister Anne (she's the religious one in the family) tells me that I am a whore. I love her dearly, but what does she know? She's twenty-eight and still a virgin. It was my own fault though. I never should have taken Alan anyplace where someone who knows me could have seen us together, but see us together Anne did, kissing and hugging, and the next day she demanded to know what I was doing. When you have been caught there is no use in denying so I told her I was spending some quality time with my lover.

"My God Marybeth! Have you forgotten you are a married woman?"

"No Anne, I haven't forgotten, although I'd very much like to."

"A lover Marybeth? You are cheating on John with a lover? Oh my God. My sister is a whore."

When she said that I lost what little 'cool' that I had and said, "Fuck you Anne" and walked away from her and hoped that she wouldn't do anything silly like tell John. He would find out soon enough, but I wanted it to be on my schedule and on my terms.

I didn't consider that I was cheating on John when I had my affair with Alan; I considered it to be revenge. It is true you know, what they say about the spouse being the last one to know. I had no idea of how long it had been going on, but long enough for everyone that John worked with to know about it. At least that is the way it seemed to me when I attended John's company Christmas party.

We were sitting at a table with John's secretary Tammy and her boyfriend and I had noticed a lot of sidelong glances directed our way and I had also noticed what I can only call 'smirks' on some of the faces that looked our way. I found out why when I went into the ladies room. There were six stalls and three of them were occupied, so I took the empty one on the far end. While I was in there, the occupants of the three that had been in used, finished their business and were at the sinks washing their hands and touching up their make up when one of them said:

"Can you believe it? John has the gall to sit his slut at the same table as his wife?"

"Tammy doesn't think she is a slut. She thinks she is the about to be the new Mrs. Bernard."

"That's what Sally thought too, until he got tired of her and fired her."

"He can be such a dick head at times."

"At times? He has been an asshole since he has been here. Remember when he fired Patty because she wouldn't go out with him?"

"I wonder if Tammy's boyfriend knows he is getting a lot of John's leftovers?"

"Oh come on Marge, say it like it is (giggle, giggle) - sloppy seconds -(giggle, giggle).

"I feel sorry for John's poor wife. She looks like she doesn't have a clue."

"Yeah, well, as much as I dislike John, I'm not going to be the one to tell her."

As they left the room, I sat there and stared at the stall door and I thought that Marge had been right - I didn't have a clue. When I got back to the table John and Tammy were gone and Tammy's boyfriend answered my unspoken question:

"They've gone to the bathroom."

Funny, I thought, I just came from there and I sure didn't see her. Maybe ten minutes later, John came back to the table and a minute or so after that Tammy reappeared. It was hard for me to do, but I managed to get through the rest of the evening without giving John or Tammy cause to suspect that I suspected something.

That night when we got home I did something that I hadn't done in our eight years of marriage - I told John I had a headache when he wanted to make love. Make love? Not bloody likely, he just wanted someone to put out the fire his lover started.

<<O>>

The party had been on a Wednesday night and when I got to work the next day I called Marsha in Legal and asked her whom we used for our fraud investigations. She gave me the number to call and the name to ask for. I called the number and asked for Alan Pendergast and they told me he was out of the office. They took my name and number and said they would page him and have him call me.

Five minutes later there was a 'knock, knock' and I looked up to see a tall, good-looking man standing in the doorway to my office.

"Mrs. Bernard?"

"Yes, may I help you?"

"Alan Pendergast. I was downstairs talking to Marge when I was paged. I recognized the number and asked Marge, who the extension belonged too and here I am. How can I be of service?"

"Unfortunately Mr. Pendergast, I find myself in need of a private investigator. I don't know if your firm handles domestic cases, but I thought that if you didn't you could recommend someone."

"Please call me Alan and yes, we do have a section that handles domestic cases. What seems to be the problem?"

I told him about the party and what I'd overheard. "It is hearsay, but they seemed very sure of themselves in what they knew. I want to be sure also."

He took down some information on John and said he would look into it. Five days later he called me:

"I'm sorry Marybeth, but those women knew what they were talking about. If you want proof that you can take into court it will take another week or so, but if all you want is to know for sure we do have an audio tape."

"How did you do that?"

"They take a room at the Motel 6 on their lunch hour and then they go back to work. After work they go back to the room for an hour or so before your husband heads for home. While they were back at work we bribed one of the cleaning ladies to let us in the room to plant a bug. Now that we know their schedule, I can get a couple of cameras in there. All I need is for you to give me the go ahead."

"Go ahead and do it Alan."

Alan dropped the audiotape of at my office later that afternoon. I debated on whether to listen to it in the car on the way home or wait until everyone was gone for the day and listen to it in my office. The last thing I needed was to lose it while listening to the tape while driving the car and hitting someone or something. I probably would have been better off if I had just taken Alan's word that John was guilty and not listened to the tape at all, but that's water under the bridge now.

When the office cleared out at five I waited ten minutes and then did a walk through the office to make sure that I was alone and then I went down to the third floor conference room and pushed the tape in the tape player.

There was the sound of a door opening and then a woman giggling and saying:

"Hurry up baby, get naked. I need that big cock of yours in me."

Next the voice of my husband said:

"I want to get it in you as bad as you want it in you."

"You have a nice hard cock baby, and I've been horny since lunchtime wanting to get it back in me."

A little laugh from John and then, "What? You don't think I haven't been rock hard all afternoon wanting to get back here?"

Sounds of clothing hitting the floor and then, "Damn Tammy, you have the hottest mouth that has ever wrapped around my cock."

"Better than your wife's?"

"Much better lover. Everything you do is much better than what she does."

"Better than that slut Sally?"

"No comparison baby, you're the best."

"I just love sucking your sweet cock."

"Jesus Tam, that feels fantastic."

There were slurping sounds, moans and then, "Oh God I'm cumming, I'm cumming."

More slurping sounds and then Tammy said, "I just had to get that one out of the way lover so with your next hard on you be able to give me a long, hard fuck."

"How do you expect me to fuck you with a dead cock?"

"Don't you sweat it baby, I'll have you back up in no time."

There were four or five minutes of moaning and sucking sounds and then Tammy said:

"Okay baby, put it in me and fuck my eyes out. Oooooh sweet fucking Jesus, that feels so good."

Then there were minutes of the sound of flesh smacking flesh, moans and gasps and sharp little cries of pleasure. "Fuck me baby, fuck me hard. Aaaaaaaaaaaghhhhh…oh yes lover, like that, hard, just like tha…Aaaaaaaaaaaahhhhhhh…oh God, oh God, oh God" Tammy squealed, "Fuck me, like that, fuck me."

"Take this" John said followed by several loud slaps of meat hitting meat and at that point I turned of the recorder. You bastard, I had thought, you miserable fucking bastard.

<<O>>

Six days later, on a Thursday, Alan stopped by my office and handed me a videotape. "There is two days worth on that tape. We bribed the desk clerk and she put them in a room we had already set up with cameras and then she made sure that they got the same room the next time they came back. You have Monday's and yesterday's meetings on that tape, both sessions, lunch and after work."

"How much do I owe you for what you've done?"

"Nada. We do one hell of a lot of business with this company and we don't mind doing the occasional favor for people who work here."

"Nonsense Alan. I have to pay for this myself. Gifts like this have a way of coming back and biting you on your butt and I'm going to need this job when I dump John."

"Okay, I'll give you an invoice. For a discount, how about having dinner with me tonight?"

"I don't know about that Alan."

"You don't want to go straight home from work in the mood you will be in because of that tape. Have dinner with me and I'll get a couple of stiff drinks in you to mellow you out a bit and then you can head on home in a tolerable mood."

Dinner was pleasant. I'd had the prime rib and we ordered a carafe of the house red and followed dinner with a Bailey's Irish Cream. After the waiter had cleared the table Alan handed me the invoice for what his firm had done. The total came to two thousand and twelve dollars and a rubber stamp had printed "Paid in full" on it.

"I can't take this Alan."

"Yes, you can. You have a receipt that says you paid in full so you are covered. We will call the pleasure of your company tonight as payment of the invoice."

I looked at him for several seconds and then I asked, "What is your company's position on helping customers get revenge?"

"What did you have in mind?"

"A little bit of what is good for the gander is good for the goose. I need someone to take up the slack."

"What do you mean by take up the slack?"

"Over the past year my sex life has gone from four, five and sometimes six times a week down to two or three times every two weeks. John has always claimed that it is because he is too tired when he gets home from work. He has been putting in ten and twelve hours a day at work, or so he claims, in order to lock up the next vice-president's slot when it opens up. He keeps telling me he is the odds on favorite to get Sam Cockneys position when Sam retires at the end of the year. He may be too tired for me when he gets home, but now we know that it isn't the job that is wearing him out. What I would like is to find a stud to get me back up to four or five times a week. How about it Alan, are you a stud?"

<<O>>

Was he ever!!! We left the restaurant and he took me to his apartment. I didn't waste any time when we got there. He asked me if I wanted a tour of the place and I said, "Just lead me to the bedroom." By the time we had reached the room, I was down to panties, thigh highs and my high heels and as I started to kick the heels off Alan said:

"Please leave them on. One of my biggest turn ons is high heels and nylons."

"You're in luck then honey, because I love the way they make my legs look and a I have a dozen pair I can wear for you."

I was stepping out of my panties as he lowered his trousers and briefs and I got a look at his cock. It wasn't any bigger - lengthwise - than John's, but it was definitely bigger around. I wasn't by any means a round-heeled slut when I met John, but I had sampled a cock or three before deciding to give my heart to John and Alan's was by far the biggest one I'd ever seen and I wondered if I could handle it. Well, I was the one who had instigated things and I sure wasn't going to back out once I was naked.

I walked over to him and reached for his cock, but he pushed my hand away and said;

"My flat so I get to go first."

He pushed me back onto the bed, pushed my legs apart and then lowered his mouth to my sex and when his tongue parted my pussy lips I felt like an electric current flowed through me and from then on it just got better and better. He licked and sucked me through two orgasms before I pushed him away and lowered my head to repay the favor. He was more than a mouthful and I'm afraid that the first time I sucked his cock he didn't get much out of it. I could barely get the head of his cock in my mouth so I wrapped my lips around the head and then I stroked him until he came in my mouth and then I swallowed every last drop. When I took my mouth off of him I said:

"It will take some getting used to your size, but I will get better at it, I promise."

"You did just fine. Most of the ladies I've gone out with would never even try."

I had my hand on his cock and I was slowly stroking it as we talked and I felt it begin to harden. I looked at him in surprise and he grinned at me and said:

"When I'm around a beautiful and sexy woman I have a fast recovery time."

He pushed me back on the bed and moved over me and I bit my lip as I waited for the pain I thought his large member would cause me, but he took his time and was surprisingly gentle as he slowly worked his way into me. He went slow until I had adjusted to his size and then he fucked me slow and steady until I started to moan and dig my nails into his back and then he picked up the pace. The louder I moaned the faster he drove into me until I had my legs wrapped around him and started begging him to fuck me harder and then he turned it loose. He fucked me fast and furious, as I moaned, cried and screamed out as I had one orgasm after another.

Alan fucked me three times before he couldn't get it up any more and then he fell to the bed next to me. In the warm afterglow Alan asked me what I planned on doing.

"Try and keep you interested since I really would like to do it again - a lot!"

"I mean what are you going to do about your situation?"

"Short term I'm going to give him what he has been giving me. I'm going to tell him that I have a chance for a promotion and that I'm going to be putting in some late hours to try and nail it down. Hopefully I'll be putting in those late hours here. Am I being too presumptuous in assuming you liked what we just did as much as I did and you would like to continue?"

"You assume correctly and yes, I most definitely would like to continue."

"Okay, short term, I'll be too tired for him on the nights he decides he wants me. Long term will be to hit him where it will hurt him the most and that is in his pocket book and his image. He is one of those who believe that he who has the most and biggest toys wins. He who has the biggest house, the most expensive car and on and on and on. I'm going to ruin his image and hurt him in the pocketbook."

"How are you going to do that?"

"I'm going to spend him into the poorhouse and trash his reputation. I may have to ask you for a favor on the reputation part."

"What?"

"If I can't find Sally and Patty, the girls he fired, I may ask you to take a shot at it."

I did find Sally and Sally told me about Rachel, the girl John got rid of so he could take up with Sally. I found Rachel and she told me where I could find Patty and then I got the three of them to sit down with me and we had a long talk. We all four agreed that John was an asshole and we came up with a plan and started working on it. If the plan worked John's reputation would be trashed.

The financial end would take a little longer to work out because it depended on some things over which I had no control. I needed John to successfully conclude the negotiations, he was working on, and get his commission check and then I needed for him to go out of town on business for three or four days.

In keeping with his penchant for having bigger and better John had long planned to install an in-ground swimming pool and have a tennis court put in. He had saved every bonus and commission check for the last two years for the purpose, and his next commission check would give him enough to do it. I'd let him finish doing it and that's when I would divorce him - after he had sunk all his money into the house and increased its value. The house would have to be sold as part of the divorce and I'd get even more out of the deal than I would have if I had gone after him when I found out about his affair with Tammy. Also, in the division of assets he would have to sell all of his toys or deduct their value from the cash assets that he would have to split with me. But all that would have to wait until John got the pool built.

There were some things that I could do while I waited for John to get the pool and tennis court done. First, I rented a storage unit and using John's credit cards started buying the things I would need when I left John and I moved those things into the storage unit.

Next, my parents had left me a mountain cabin on six acres and while I had always meant to add John's name to the title I had never gotten around to doing it so it was in my name only. According to the attorney I talked to, it was not a jointly acquired asset, so it would be excluded from the divorce settlement. The cabin had a marvelous view of the south side of Pike's Peak, but the place had some drawbacks. It was strictly a weekend get-a-way kind of place. It didn't have water - we had to carry water in - and it had no electricity or phone. I decided to rectify that. Mundane chores like paying the bills were beneath John so I pretty much handled all of our finances. We had several certificates of deposit that were supposed to be part of our retirement portfolio and I cashed them in and used the money to have a well drilled and a power line run to the cabin. Those two actions alone tripled the value of the place. Next I had the outhouse removed and a septic field put in, brought in a contractor and had the cabin wired and a flush toilet installed. John never knew about any of that because he never went up to the cabin in the winter or spring. He wouldn't go up there until about mid-June or so and by then I hoped to have shoved Tammy up his ass.

<<O>>

John got his commission check and started on the pool and

tennis court. My life with John was basically one of co-existence. He was "working hard" to get his promotion and I was "working" just as hard to get mine and we hadn't had sex in almost three months. Not that I missed it - Alan was taking very good care of me - but I could tell that John was irritated by my always being 'too tired' to make love. A couple of times he got snappy with me about it and I reminded him of all the times he was too tired to take care of my needs.

"It will get better" I told him, "Another two months at the most and I'll have my promotion."

He whined that I really didn't need the promotion, that he was perfectly capable of supporting me.

"It isn't the money John, it is the prestige and the knowing that I'm just that much better than the others that wanted the promotion."

There was no promotion so it was all bullshit of course, but since that is the way John thought he bought it.

Two weeks after the pool and tennis court were finished John had a pool party and invited a host of friends, neighbors and people that he and I worked with. Tammy was there and she was just so nice to me that it was sickening, but I smiled all the way through the party. I made sure that I was always close to where she was or where John was so they couldn't sneak off together. I didn't want John to get laid because I had plans for him.

Alan was at the party, but he acted no different towards me than any of my co-workers who were at the party, although a couple of times when he caught my eye he winked at me and my knees went weak at the thought of what I had planned. I gave John and Tammy just enough room that Tammy could get John all hot and bothered, but still stayed close enough to keep anything from happening.

The party started breaking up around eleven and a frustrated Tammy was among the first to leave. As soon as she was gone, I nodded my head toward Alan and we left the room separately and met at the laundry room. I quickly pulled off my panties and bent over the washing machine and Alan moved behind me. I was so wet from anticipation (plus being used to him by then) that he slid his full length into me with the first push. It was a fast and furious no frills fuck, but that is all we had time for. He brought me to an orgasm and shortly after that he came in me. He pulled out, I quickly pulled on my panties, gave him a passionate kiss and then we hurried back to the dying party.

Half an hour later everyone was gone and I was alone with my husband. I took him by the hand and led him to the bedroom.

"No excuses from either of us tonight John. It has been too long and I need some sex. I've spent all day waiting for this moment and I'm hot, wet and ready to explode."

He was also hot, Tammy had seen to that, so he offered no resistance when I undressed him, pushed him back on the bed and mounted him. I didn't even undress; I just pulled off my panties, swung over him and lowered myself down onto his erection. As he slid into me, I smiled, knowing that I was giving him sloppy seconds. I started moving up and down on him coating his cock with Alan's juices and I rode him hard until I got him to cum. As soon as he squirted into me, I cried out:

"No baby, no. I'm almost there baby, don't stop now, get me off baby, get me off."

And then John did what I hoped he would do - he moved so that he could eat my pussy. As soon as his tongue entered me and he started licking up the juices flowing from my pussy I had a mind-blowing orgasm. It went on and on fueled by the knowledge that my cheating ass husband was sucking my lover's cum out of me. True, it was diluted by some of John's cum, but John was still sucking Alan out of me. I kept my fingers clutched in his hair until the orgasms faded and then I yawned and rolled over and pretended to go to sleep, leaving John with the hard on he had developed while eating me. Sweet Jesus, did it ever feel good to do that to him.

What I had been waiting for happened two weeks after the pool party. John told me he would be flying to Chicago on Monday for a four-day business trip and that he expected to be named a vice-president when he returned.

"Oh Jesus baby," I said, "That will be perfect. I expect that everything I've been working toward will happen by the time you get back."

"That's great" John said, "We can have a big celebration."

"Oh, I plan on celebrating baby, you can depend on it."

I had everything in place when John flew home on Friday. I wished I could have seen his face when he saw his shiny new Hummer when he got to the parking lot. Someone had slashed all four tires and had keyed both sides and the hood down to bare metal. While he stood there and screamed obscenities at the unknown vandals two men who had been parked there waiting for him got out of their car, walked over to him and served him with the divorce papers and the restraining order keeping him away from me and the house. John was not a stupid man and I know he put two and two together and came up with who had trashed his prize Hummer - two men waiting there for him had to be a tip off - but he had no proof.

It was mid-afternoon by the time he got the arrangements made to have the Hummer picked up and taken to the dealership and got the police report out of the way. He made three cell phone calls to me that I refused to answer and he was not in the best of moods when he reached his office. Things did not improve any for him when he got there. First of all Tammy wasn't sitting at her desk and he didn't know the woman who was sitting there. He asked where Tammy was and the woman said she didn't know. All she knew was that she was supposed to tell John to report to Mr. Everett's office as soon as he arrived.

John headed for Bert's office expecting to be congratulated on closing the Falcon deal and be told he was the new vice-president. Instead he found out that he didn't even have a job. At ten that morning Bert had been served with papers informing him that the company was being sued by Sally, Patty and Rachel for sexual harassment and wrongful termination due to their refusal to grant John sexual favors (not exactly true since Sally and Rachel had let John in their pants), but that would only come out in court and we were expecting the company to settle long before it got on a court docket.

At ten-thirty that morning a special messenger delivered a package to Bert and it contained video captures of John and Tammy engaged in sexual practices. Bert called Tammy in and she broke down, cried and told Bert that John had threatened to fire her if she didn't put out for him. Wisely Bert did not fire Tammy although we had hoped he would so we could make her part of the sexual harassment suit. John however was a different story. He was told to have his office cleared out and to be out of the building in an hour.

Since the restraining order kept him from coming home, he had to check into a motel and over the next three days he found out that all of his credit cards had been maxed out or cancelled, there was no money in the checking or savings accounts and the safe deposit box were empty. The crowning touch was when the insurance company told him that they weren't going to cover the damage to his Hummer. I had cancelled the insurance a week before he left on his trip.

Alan and I had been extremely careful (except for the one time Anne saw us) and John had nothing he could use to counter sue. Since there were no children the divorce moved along quick. John was pushing for a sixty/forty split of the assets based on the fact that he was the major breadwinner. My attorney fought for a seventy-five/twenty-five split since there wouldn't be a divorce if he hadn't become an unfaithful husband. John was on unemployment and strapped for funds - he didn't even have a car to go job hunting until he could come up with the money to get his Hummer back - so he had a choice to make. He could negotiate and settle or he could wait it out and go in front of a judge and see how the judge would rule. I think his lawyer convinced him that he would get the short end of the stick if he went in front of a judge so he settled for a sixty/forty split in my favor.

The house and all of John's toys - the boat and trailer, the dirt bikes, the ATV's and snowmobiles had to be sold and all the money had to be thrown into the pot to be split sixty/forty between us. Part of my deal with Sally and Rachel when I fronted them the money, was for the attorney, so that they could sue John's company and they wouldn't sue John personally until our divorce was final. The day after the divorce was final they sued John personally for sexual harassment and wrongful termination. Their lawyer petitioned the court to freeze John's assets pending the outcome of the suit. My attorney said there wasn't much chance of a judge ordering it, but John still had to pay an attorney to fight it and that is what it was all about for me - killing John financially.

But what really killed John was to see me still living in his house and knowing that I was enjoying the pool, tennis court and hot tub. I had improved the cabin that my parents had left me. I had sold it and given the money to Alan, who added some of his money and used it to buy the house.

Alan bought the house as an agent of the MFJ Investment Company and at the closing as John and I were signing the papers Alan said that MFJ was buying the house as an income property and he asked me if I would like to rent the house and continue living there. The look on John's face when I said yes was priceless. In a couple of months I will let John know that MFJ only has two stock holders, me and Alan and that the initials MFJ stand for Marybeth Fucks John.

Alan and I are to be married next month and I'm wondering if I should invite Anne to the wedding or not.

End of the 5th story

Nan's Boyfriends

I knew something was up because Nan had been fidgety since I walked in the front door. It was one of the signs that she had something to say that she didn't think I was going to like to hear. After fifteen years of marriage I knew the signs and I also knew that I couldn't hurry things along. When Nan had something like that to say she had to work herself up to say it. So, while I waited for her to finish dinner, I grabbed a beer and went into the living room to watch CNN.

When Nan called me for dinner, I was surprised to see that she had opened a couple of bottles of wine, one on the table and one on the sideboard to 'breathe,' and she had already poured two glasses. Since we rarely had wine with our meals during the week I asked her what was the occasion.

"I'm trying to get you in a mellow mood."

"In other words I'm not going to like what's coming, am I?"

"Probably not."

"Well, why not just go ahead and get it over with?"

"Not yet. Wait until we finish the wine."

"That bad?"

Nan looked down at her wine glass and said, "Pretty bad."

We sat in silence as we finished dinner and I wondered what 'pretty bad' could mean.

When dinner was over and the dishes were cleared away, I said, "Living room, family room, bedroom or here?"

"Here is fine" and she got up and got the other bottle of wine off the sideboard. She refilled our glasses and then she sat down across from me.

"Would you say we have a good marriage?"

"I would say we have an excellent marriage."

"Are you happy with me?"

"Of course I am."

"You do know that I love you, don't you?"

"Yes, I believe I do, now what's this all about?"

She watched me silently for several moments, took a big gulp of her wine and then she said, "One of my boyfriends wants to take me to Cancun this weekend for a week and I want to go."

My wine glass was halfway to my mouth before what Nan had said registered on me. I put the glass down on the table and stared at her not believing what I had heard and not knowing what to say. I just sat there and stared at her.

"Aren't you going to say anything?"

"Say what? Start where? The sudden news that you had a boyfriend would have floored me, but boyfriends plural? I don't know what to say. When, why, how long, how many, why are you telling me this, what do you expect me to say? If you need to hear me say something how about this - just how long past the end of this conversation do you expect this marriage to last? For that matter, why are we even having this conversation? Why don't you just pack your bags and head for Cancun? It's a damned good bet that I won't be here when you get back anyway."

"That's what this is all about honey. I want you here when I get back. I won't even go unless you say I can."

"You can't be that stupid Nan. Whether you go or not doesn't matter. You have just informed me that you have been cheating on me. You are unfaithful - you are fucking other men behind my back. You think I'm just going to sit here and say "That's nice dear, and have you been having a good time?" We don't need to say anymore; you've just said all that needs to be said. The marriage is toast. Go to fucking Cancun. Go anywhere you fucking want to, it doesn't matter to me any more."

I got up from the table and headed for the basement.

"Where are you going?"

"To get a suitcase."

"Why?"

"Because I'm getting out of here and I'm going to need to pack some things."

"Please stay and talk to me honey."

"We have nothing to talk about."

"Yes, we do. We need to talk about us."

"God damn it Nan, there is no more 'us'. We stopped being an 'us' when you hit me with that boyfriend shit. Just leave me alone."

I went to the basement and got a couple of suitcases and went up to the bedroom to pack. Nan stood in the doorway and watched me for several minutes and then she turned and walked away. I finished packing and carried the suitcases out to the car and put them in the trunk. When I got in the car I found Nan sitting on the passenger side. She looked over at me and said, "I'm sticking to you like glue until we talk this out. You admitted that we had a great marriage. You said you were happy with me and you acknowledged that you believe that I love you. So I've had lovers, so what? Our marriage has still been great and I still love you so at least hear me out before you take off."

"All right, go ahead and talk."

"Please honey, just come back inside. We can sit at the kitchen table where I can sip my wine. I need the wine to help me say what I need to say and I'm going to need it to keep me going."

She took a sip of the Merlot and then said, "First off, I have to say that I love you with all my heart. I love being married to you, I love going to sleep in your arms and I love waking up with you cuddled up next to me. I love everything about you; your laugh, your tenderness and I love the way you make me feel. I love the way you make love to me and that is where the problem with me is. You just don't do it often enough."

I started to say something, but Nan held up her hand, "Please let me finish - let me get it all out - and then you can say whatever you want or ask any questions you want to." She took another sip of her wine; "You don't need sex as much as I do, honey. You are fantastic in bed and you never fail to make my toes curl when we make love, but honey, you just don't want sex all that often. For the last six years you have been happy with once, sometimes twice a week and that isn't near enough for me. Where once a week is good enough for you I could handle once or twice a day."

She took another sip of her wine.

"Back when we slowed down to once or twice a week I spent a small fortune on sexy under things and sexy high heels to try and get you in the mood to make love more often, but you never seemed to notice. I tried being more aggressive in instigating things, but you never responded. Eventually I came to understand that you just weren't all that interested in sex. In all other things you and I were perfect for each other and our marriage was great so I resigned myself to only having sex when you were ready. That lasted about two months and by the end of that two months I was so sexually frustrated that I got irritable and cranky and we started having all those arguments over piddily little shit that didn't amount to much and it was putting a hell of a strain on our marriage. I don't think the marriage would have survived another six months if I hadn't had too much to drink at your sisters wedding shower."

She got up and opened another bottle of wine and when she went to pour me some I waved her away. She refilled her own glass and said, "The girls had all chipped in to hire a male stripper to come in and perform. The girls were pretty raunchy that night and they were tossing him money to try and get him to strip down all the way and when he finally did and I saw his hard cock sticking out in front of him I started to feel sorry for myself. It just so happened that he left the party a minute after I did and he saw me having trouble putting the key in the car door lock. I was crying so hard that I could hardly see. He came over to help me and one thing led to another and I ended up at his apartment and in his bed. He screwed me five times before I had to leave and come home. I was fine after that. Oh, I did feel guilty and I cried a lot over the fact that I had betrayed your trust, but the frustration was gone, the irritability was gone and so was the crankiness. But it came back and so did the arguments and the arguments were getting worse. One day we had one that left me so angry that I just wanted to scream and run through the house breaking things. I was cleaning out my purse and I found the piece of paper that Chad had given me with his number on it. I had forgotten that he had given it to me. I was just mad enough at you that day to call him and when he invited me over I went. From then on I saw him three and four times a week. Things smoothed out in our marriage, I was happy and I was able to keep you happy. I know that doesn't make it right, but it worked."

"Six years? You have been doing this six years and have been able to hide it from me?"

"I did it during the day while you were at work and I always made sure I was home and cleaned up well before you got home. There wasn't any way for you to have found out."

"So I don't satisfy you."

"That's not what I said honey. You always satisfied me when we made love. You just don't do it often enough."

"So what you are telling me is that you are a slut for cock and you have a stable of studs to see that you get it."

"I guess you could put it that way, at least from your point of view."

"How would you put it?"

"I would say that I have a few friends that help me out in my hour of need."

"Just how many is a few?"

"Three or four."

"You don't even know for sure?"

"It changes. It started out as just Chad. Then Chad graduated and got a job in another city. He introduced me to Tony, another dancer he worked with, and then Tony moved, and I met Gary. Chad moved back to town and I dated both Gary and Chad for a while and then Tony moved back and it just keeps changing. Right now I'm seeing Chad, Harry, Rudy and Glenn, but Harry is supposed to be moving to Dallas this week. I don't see them all at once, I just take turns dating them. That way I avoid any emotional entanglements."

"So who is it who wants to take you to Cancun?"

"Chad."

"And just what is it that makes this Chad think that you can come and just ask me to let you take off for a week with him?"

"He doesn't know I'm asking you."

"Then what in Christ's name made you think you could do it without causing our marriage to self destruct?"

"Try to understand this honey. I'm gambling here. I know I love you and I was sure that you loved me. What I have been doing for the last six years has not affected your quality of life one little bit. If anything, what I've been doing has made things better for us because we don't argue and fight anymore. But circumstances change. My boyfriends are losing the ability to see me during the day when we are relatively free from worrying about being found out. To continue to get the sexual satisfaction that I need I'm going to have to do it in the evenings which almost guarantees that I will eventually get caught. So I decided to bite the bullet and out myself. I'm gambling that I can convince you that I love you more that anything, that you haven't lost anything and that you won't lose anything if I continue. If I can't convince you then the marriage is over. If I hadn't come forward now and I'd have been caught the marriage still would have been over. I'm hoping that by doing it this way I'll have a chance at keeping you."

"I don't see how Nan. As long as I didn't know we could have kept on going, but now I do know. I'd never be able to come home again without wondering who you spent the day with and what you did. I'd never be able to kiss you again without thinking about where that mouth had been and what it had been doing. Just the thought that I've been kissing you after you have sucked some other man's cock, is making my stomach turn right now. Look at the bright side. Now you can fuck your stable all day and all night every day. That should keep you sexually satisfied."

She looked at me with tears in her eyes, "Damn it Ben, I love you and I don't want you to leave me."

"Sorry Nan, you should have thought of that before you let yourself become a slut."

<<O>>

I spent the next three days in a motel wondering just how in the hell that a marriage that had been so good for fifteen years could have gone down the chute so quickly. I loved Nan and it killed me to be away from her, but I also knew I was right when I stated the way I would feel when I would come home to her. She professed love for me, but how could she expect me to kiss her knowing that she had just sucked another man's cock? How could she expect me to sit across from her at the dinner table knowing that just a couple of hours earlier, she had been on her back with her legs spread for some other guy? After fifteen years she had to know me better than that.

Sitting in the motel and staring at the TV, I thought about Nan's reason for doing what she did. She was right that I didn't seem to need a lot of sex, but I wasn't going to accept that it was my fault that she turned herself into a whore. There were plenty of women in the world whose husbands were like me and they didn't go out whoring. So I only made love once or twice a week, what was wrong with that? When it happened I was making love not having sex, and it wasn't any quick coupling either - it sometimes lasted an hour or more and it was almost always more than once or twice. I sometimes went three and four times. What was wrong with having quality instead of quantity? I loved Nan and I do believe that she loved me, but Jesus - how could she expect me to live with what she had become?

My car needed work, so I dropped it off at the dealership on a Saturday morning and took a cab over to my house. Nan would be in Cancun with her asshole and I could take my time going through the place and packing up what I wanted. I held the cab long enough to check the garage and make sure Nan's car was gone. It was so I paid off the cab driver and then let myself inside the house. About an hour later, I was in the bedroom taking clothes out of the closet when I heard the garage door opener start up. At the same time, I heard a car door slam out in the drive and when I went to the window and looked out I saw a man getting out of a pickup truck. The shock of seeing the man rattled me more than I cared to admit. Nan had said nothing about the fact that one of her lovers was black.

Obviously Nan had brought one of her lovers to the house and the last thing I wanted was a confrontation with Nan and one of her assholes so I quickly shoved the boxes I'd packed in the closet and closed the door. I hurried down the hall to the spare bedroom. As soon as the two of them were in the master bedroom I would get out of the house. I heard them coming up the stairs and then I heard the man say, "Isn't that your bedroom?"

"Yes, but we aren't going to use it."

"Why not?"

"Because that bedroom is mine and Ben's."

"What does that mean? The idiot left you."

"Yes, but I'm hoping that he will come back someday and I would feel bad if he did and I'd used the room with someone else. It's bad enough that I polluted his wife, I can't do it to his room too."

Shit! They were coming to the spare bedroom. I quickly got into the closet and I'd just made it as the two of them came through the door. I wasn't even able to close the closet door because they would have heard the click of the latch. The man was talking, "I still don't understand why you wouldn't go to Cancun with me this weekend. Your husband left you, you're free to do what you want."

"I told you. Ben might come home and I want to be here if he does."

"What if you get your wish and he comes home while I'm here? Won't that just make it worse?"

"I know Ben. If he gets over his mad it won't be for days. Besides, if he comes by he'll see your truck and he will just keep on going. He all ready knows that even if we get back together, I am going to keep on seeing you guys."

The two of them were undressing as they were talking and the man said, "You aren't making sense Nan."

"That goes with being in love Chad. I love Ben and it tends to cloud my thinking."

Nan pushed Chad back on the bed and knelt between his legs and when I saw that white on black I got an immediate hard on. I don't know what sick thing in my mind made it happen, but happen it did. Taking Chad's black stick in her white hand, she began stroking it as she said, "Haven't you ever been in love Chad? If you had you would know how stupid things can get."

"I'm in love, but so far it's been hopeless."

"Why is that?"

"She's married and in love with her husband."

"Poor baby. No hope at all?"

"I don't know, you tell me."

Nan stopped stroking his cock and looked up at him. She looked at him in silence for several seconds and then said, "That's sweet baby, but I'm sorry. I belong to Benny and always will, even if he doesn't come back. Try and settle for what you have baby, but know that it is all you are ever going get" and then she lowered her head toward his cock. When that black pole disappeared into her white mouth, my cock actually throbbed.

For the next two hours I was stuck in the closet as Nan and Chad had sex on the bed in front of me. They did it all, several times, and it was like watching a porno movie, but without the horrible music in the background. She sucked his cock and then he fucked her. They went sixty-nine and then he fucked her again. Then he went down on her and sucked his own cum out of her pussy and he seemed to enjoy it. I wondered why I had never tried it because Nan certainly seemed to love it.

The black and white thing was so erotic that more than anything I wanted to take out my hard cock and beat myself off, but I didn't dare do anything that might call attention to the closet so I just stood there and suffered.

On the bed Nan got on her knees and buried her head in a pillow and Chad took her in her ass. That was something else I had never done and something else that Nan seemed to love. When Chad finally came, he pulled out of her ass, and fell to the bed beside her. Nan rolled over and laid next to him and said, "You sure do know how to make a girl feel good."

"You should give some thought to making it permanent."

"I'm sorry baby, but it will never happen. I share my body with you, but my heart belongs to Ben and if he comes back I'll be here waiting for him even if it takes twenty years."

"Well, I'm going to keep trying, but for now I have my sister's birthday party to go to. When can I see you again?"

"I don't know baby. Give me a call on Tuesday."

Nan laid on the bed and watched Chad dress and when he was done, she got up and walked him to the front door. I came out of the closet to listen at the door and see what Nan would do next. I was hoping that she would shower, which would give me a chance to get out of the house. I heard the front door close and then I heard her coming back up the stairs. I had the door opened just a crack so I could see and when she got to the head of the stairs she didn't go into our bedroom. She stopped at the linen closet and got out some sheets and I suddenly realized that she was going to make up the bed that she and Chad had just messed up. I quickly got back in the closet and watched as Nan came in and stripped the bed and then remade it. When she was done, she sat down on the bed and looked toward the closet, "You might as well come out Ben, I know you are in there. I caught a glimpse of you when I got out of bed to walk Chad out."

I stepped out of the closet and headed for the bedroom door and Nan said, "Were you peeping intentionally?"

I told her no and I told her how I'd come to be in the closet and why the door hadn't been fully closed.

"Well, now you've seen just how big a slut I can be. I hope it wasn't a shock to your system."

"Let's just say that it was eye opening."

"It had to be something to give you that bulge in your pants. Let me guess - was it because he was black, or was it when he took my ass?"

"That and when he ate you after cumming in you."

"Well Ben, you always could have done either of those things, but you just never seemed to interested in the kinky side of sex. It's still there if you want it."

"No thanks," I said as I headed for the door.

"Are you sure you won't stay for a while Ben? At least long enough for me to take care of your problem?"

I just shook my head no as I walked out the bedroom door and left the house.

The rest of the weekend was pretty much shot as far as I was concerned. It didn't matter what I did I couldn't get Nan and her black lover and what they did out of my mind. Wherever I looked, I saw Nan's white hands on the back of Chad's black head, pulling his face into her cum filled pussy. I saw her head buried in the pillow and I heard her moans as Chad pushed his black cock into Nan's tight white ass. I saw them sixty-nine as I was trying to watch Fox News. I saw Nan on her knees with her head bobbing up and down on Chad's cock when I tried to watch the football game.

It was like that all weekend and it was even like that when I tried to sleep. Saturday I had one dream where Nan was in a room with four black men and she was tugging on their cocks and saying "Eeny, meeny, miney moe" to choose the boyfriend who would fuck her for the next week. That dream faded and was replaced by one where Nan was standing on a street corner with a sign that said, "Need boyfriend to fuck me because my husband won't. Black only need to apply." Sunday I had the "Eeny meeny" dream again, only this time Nan couldn't choose so she told them all to follow her into the bedroom. Then I followed and tried to peek into the room and someone slammed the door in my face. I didn't get much sleep all that weekend and when I woke up Monday morning I was a wreck.

Monday at work I was a zombie. I attended two meetings and took part in a conference call and I don't remember anything from any of them. Tuesday was no better and by Wednesday I began to think that I had better put in for some time off to get my head back together before I got fired. Wednesday evening I left work and headed for my motel room and the next thing I knew I was in front of my house. I hadn't planned on being there, but there I was. There were two strange vehicles in the driveway and I knew what that meant so I drove on by. I steered the car back toward the motel, but ten minutes later I was still in the neighborhood after driving several times around the block. I must have driven around the block seven or eight times before I stopped in front and parked at the curb. I had no idea why I was there, but I sat in my car and stared at the house for about five minutes before something made me get out of the car and go into the house.

I heard noises from upstairs and I stood at the bottom of the steps and just stared up them. I knew what the noises were and I didn't want to listen to them, but suddenly I was standing at the top of the stairs with no memory of even going up them. The noises were coming from the spare bedroom and I desperately wanted to turn away and run from the house, but some unseen force was either pushing me or pulling me down the hallway to the spare bedroom door. I knew what I was going to see when I got there and I knew that I didn't want to see it, but I couldn't make myself turn around and go.

There were two black men in the room with Nan, neither one of them Chad, and they were both using her at the same time. One was lying on the bed and Nan's head was bobbing up and down in his lap. The second man was behind her. He had his hands on her hips and was holding her as he fucked her. I stood there for almost three minutes watching what was taking place on the bed and the three of them never even noticed me. I didn't want to watch, but I couldn't make myself move away. Finally the man fucking her from behind said, "Here it comes sweetie" and he rammed into hard a couple of more times and then just buried himself to the hilt and held himself there. After a bit he pulled back and his soft cock plopped out of Nan and the three of them started to change positions and noticed me. The two men saw me first and their sudden hesitancy made Nan look up. Her eyes met mine and held them as she said, "Pay him no mind. It's just my husband and he doesn't love me anymore. He's probably just here to pick up some of his stuff."

Her eyes never left mine as she rolled over onto her back and spread her legs. She reached up and pulled the man who had been in her mouth down to her and still looking into my eyes said, "Put it in me baby. You haven't come yet so put it in and fuck me. Make me scream baby, make me cum." The man shoved his cock into her and she moaned and her legs came up and locked around him. Then Nan winked at me - she actually winked at me - and said, "Get your cock over here Tony, I think my hubby likes watching." The other man walked over and got on the bed and knelt with his limp cock just over Nan's mouth. She raised up and captured it and Tony leaned down so she could take in more of him and her eyes finally left mine as she gave herself to the two men.

I didn't know what was wrong with me. I couldn't make myself move out of that doorway. I just stood there and watched as the two black men took turns stuffing their cocks into Nan's mouth and pussy. I don't know how much longer I would have stood there if Nan hadn't gotten up from the bed and come over and pulled me into the room. She told Tony to drag a chair over and put it next to the bed and then she sat me down in it.

"You can see better from here honey. Tony is going to fuck my ass next and from here you will be able to get a good look at his nice black cock as it goes into my tight, white butt."

Nan got back on the bed and put her head down on a pillow and Tony moved up behind her. She was looking into my eyes and I saw her wince just a bit and then smile as Tony pushed his cock into her ass. "God Ben, but that does feel good. Watch his cock Ben. Watch that nice piece of black meat slide in and out of my ass. Come on Tony, fuck my ass hard. Put on a show for Ben." Tony was all the way in Nan now and he started to fuck her and she moaned in pleasure. Tony plowed her ass for almost five minutes and Nan's moans became louder and longer until finally she screamed and her body shook. She fell forward on the bed and Tony's cock popped out of her ass and I saw the cum dripping off the end of it. Nan was lying on the bed, breathing hard as she tried to catch her breath. When her eyes opened and she sat up, "Thanks guys, I really needed that, but you need to leave now. I think Ben and I need some time alone."

As the two men dressed Nan got off the bed and came over to me. She knelt in front of me and unzipped my pants and took out my hard cock and she looked up at me and smiled. "Your cock is nice and hard Ben. I knew it would be. I know something about you Ben, something that you didn't even know about yourself. I knew it the day you saw Chad and me and then came out of the closet with a hard cock in your pants. You get turned on watching me fuck. Isn't that right Ben? Isn't that why your cock is so hard right now? Because you've been watching me fuck? You can deny it if you want Ben, but I know. I've got the proof right here in my hand. I've had someone here everyday since you saw me with Chad just waiting for you to come back." She lowered her head and took my cock in her mouth and I exploded. The suddenness of it took Nan by surprise and she jerked her head back and looked up at me as my cock sprayed her tits. "Oh baby. I knew you got turned on watching me, but I had no idea that it made you this hot."

She turned her head, "Hey Tony, don't leave yet."

Tony, who had been heading for the door, turned and came back, "What you need sweets?'

"I need you to fuck me again. Ass or pussy, I don't care, but I need you to fuck me while I suck Ben's cock."

Tony dropped his pants and under shorts and moved up behind Nan. I did not want to be there. I wanted to get up and run from the room, but I couldn't and I don't know why. Nan had my limp cock in her hand when Tony said, "Here it comes sweets" and he pushed forward. Nan moaned and my cock shot up. Nan looked up at me, "Oh baby, we are going to have so much fun together" and she took my cock in my mouth and started to suck it.

End of the 6th Story

Aggie's Condition

There is wife watching and then there is wife watching. They sound the same, but they are way different. The first one, for example, is watching your wife spread herself for someone else while you either participate or hide in the closet. The second one is watching someone else's wife do the same thing while hiding in the closet. I've done both and I loved doing both; I just hope that I'll be able to do it again.

I've been watching my wife Aggie (don't dare call her Agnes) for years now, sometimes from the closet, sometimes from a chair next to the bed, and sometimes I'm in one hole while someone else is in another. I found out early on in our marriage that no one man was ever going to be enough for Aggie. Remember the ugly duckling story? One day an ugly little thing and the next day a beautiful swan? That is similar to Aggie in that one day she was a virgin and the day after we consummated our marriage vows she was a nymphomaniac.

We weren't married three weeks when I came home one day and found her in bed with not one man, but three, and this following a night where she had fucked me four times, including once just before I left for work in the morning. I had ordered some furniture and I was supposed to pay the balance when the stuff was delivered and I had gone to work and had forgotten to leave the checkbook at home for Aggie. I rushed home with the checkbook and when I got there I found that the furniture had already arrived. I walked into the house and found three guys fucking Aggie, one in each available hole.

When I walked in cocks began to wilt and there was much reaching for clothes. Aggie cried out, "Don't make them stop baby, I need it, please don't stop them." I was mad, angry, pissed, call it what you will, but the pitiful tone of Aggie's voice got to me. I handed her the checkbook and went back to work. I found out later that all three guys got fired for fucking Aggie, She kept them most of the day and they actually got fired for missing all their deliveries, but to me that's the same as getting fired for fucking Aggie. As a bonus, at least from my perspective, they forgot to take the check for the furniture and my amount due got lost somewhere in the shuffle.

When I got home that night, Aggie was a bundle of nerves, "I know you hate me, but I just can't help myself. I've got to have it baby, I need it."

I hadn't been gone from the house for half an hour and she had gone into the kitchen and had gotten a cucumber and was fucking herself with it when the furniture movers got there. She had answered the door in her bathrobe, showed them where she wanted things and had then gone back into the bedroom to her cucumber. She was lying naked on the bed working the vegetable around in her pussy when she heard, "Jesus!" She looked up and found one of the delivery guys standing there staring at her pussy. She had thrown the cucumber away, spread her legs, and I had walked in on the result.

Then she confessed to me that this wasn't the first time she had been unfaithful. Her first was when we were on our honeymoon. I had gone out to see about renting a car and while I was gone, she fucked the room service waiter. Before we'd left, she'd had the bellboy, the bell captain, the waiter twice more and one cab driver in the back seat of his cab. Since moving into the house, she had fucked the cable installer, the telephone installer, the mailman (every day for the last week) and the newspaper boy. This last worried me the most since I wasn't sure of his age and she could go to jail over that.

As I listened to her run down her list of infidelities I wondered just what in the hell I was going to do. Aggie was gorgeous, could cook like a master French chef, kept a spotless house, and was the most fantastic piece of ass I'd ever had, but what could I do about the fact that she couldn't stay off her back and keep her legs closed. The bottom line was that I adored Aggie and I was just going to have to learn to cope with her "condition".

The solution was simplicity itself, at least for Aggie and me, although I did have some trouble selling the idea to some others. I approached several of my friends and asked them if they would like to fuck my wife. You would be surprised at how many said no. Not that they wouldn't have fucked her behind my back (and some of them did), but they ran scared when I asked them straight out. I finally found enough guys to agree and I set up a schedule so that Monday through Friday at least two guys would show up every day and help Aggie keep her "condition" under control. I would have to cover the evenings and the weekends.

This arrangement worked fine for about two years during which Aggie never slowed down, not even a little bit, and I finally had to cry out "enough!" I just couldn't keep up with her. That's when we began the watching. We would go out on Saturday and Sunday and Aggie would pick up some guy and we would take him home with us and Aggie would fuck his socks off.

The problem we found is that over half of the guys she picked up couldn't function when I was there, so we started sending Aggie out on her own. When she found someone she would call me and I would hide in the closet. Why? Because she wanted me around in case she hooked up with some weirdo. It turned out that I liked watching Aggie be a nympho.

After five years of marriage Aggie began to slow down some. As her daytime lovers began to fall by the wayside, we didn't bother to replace them. Soon she was down to only four lovers during the week, with me taking care of the evenings, and she also had her regular outings on Saturday and Sunday.

And then my life got complicated. Brea was our next door neighbor and had been for the last three years. Like Aggie, Brea was a stay at home wife and she and Aggie got to know each other real well and became the best of friends. It was inevitable that Brea would notice the constant comings and goings of Aggie's male friends during the day and then came the day when Brea felt she knew Aggie well enough to ask her what was going on. Aggie, in turn, felt that she knew Brea well enough to tell her the story. Brea was surprised and then she told Aggie that she envied her. Brea had also been a virgin when she married and she had always wondered what she had missed by not trying a cock or two before marriage. "I've always wondered what other men might be like. I've read books and magazines and seen lots of pictures and they all look so different."

Aggie asked her why she'd never tried a different cock and Brea had said, "Oh goodness, I wouldn't know how to."

Aggie told her to get dressed up and go out to a bar and let herself be picked up, but Brea said that she just couldn't do something like that. The two of them talked about it for weeks and finally there came a day when Brea's husband had to go out of town for several days. Aggie talked Brea into going out with her on one of her Saturday night jaunts, but Brea said she would only do it on one condition. I was in the basement working on a rocking chair when Aggie came downstairs,

"Honey, I need a favor." She explained to me that she was going to take Brea out with her that night, "But the poor dear is scared that things might not go right and she might try to back out at the last minute. She's afraid of what the guy might do to her if that happens. Would you hide in her closet in case she needs some help? Please?"

Now watching Aggie was one thing; I went along with her escapades because I didn't want to lose her, but hide in Brea's closet? I didn't think so. After several more pleases and pretty pleases and a "please do it for me baby" I gave in.

"What about you? What if you need protecting and I'm hiding in Brea's closet?"

"I'll be all right. I'll make sure I bring home someone I all ready know. So will Brea. I'll make sure she gets someone nice, but she needs the added security of knowing help is there if needed."

Which is how I found myself in Brea's closet that night watching her trembling form being slowly undressed by a guy I recognized as one of Aggie's lovers. As layer after layer of Brea's clothes came off, I began to be glad that I'd agreed to be her protector. I'd always known she was attractive, but in the loose clothing she always wore I'd never imagined that she could have such a nice body. I'd guess her to be 36-24-34 and my hard on agreed with me. At this point, I need to say that regardless of Aggie's wanderings, I'd never broken my marriage vows, but that night, seeing a naked Brea, I was willing to shatter them all to hell. I watched as Brea was seduced and then fucked by her lover of the evening. At first she was tentative and unsure, but as the night progressed she loosened up and finally she was an insatiable slut. He fucked her, she sucked his cock, he fucked her, she sucked his cock again and when he went to mount her again she rolled over and said in a little girl voice, "In my ass, I want you to do my ass."

Two hours later, he left and I was standing in the closet with my cock in my hand and with cum splashed all over the inside of the closet door and puddling on the carpet. The door opened and there stood Brea. She took one look at me and said, "Oh you poor baby. Did I do that to you? Here, let me help you with that."

An hour later, I called home and asked Aggie if her gentleman friend was still there. When she said that he was, I told her that she could invite him to stay the night and that I would see her in the morning. Brea then proceeded to demonstrate her newfound sexual prowess.

I was not prepared for the icy reception that I got when I went home in the morning. Sounding every bit the betrayed wife, Aggie greeted me with, "And just what were you doing all night?"

I explained to her what had happened and that I'd stayed and spent the night with Brea.

"How could you? How could you cheat on me with that woman?"

I was caught flat-footed by that one. "Me cheating on you? I've never touched another woman before last night, even though I've watched you parade men through our bedroom by platoons, and you're getting upset with me?"

"That's different and you know it! I need more than you can give me, but it's not the same for you. Anytime you have a hard on I want it and I'm ready for it. You don't have to go some place else to get it like I do."

I guess that's what they call female logic; anyway, Aggie stayed pissed at me for all of two hours and then she needed to be fucked again and suddenly I was forgiven. Poor Brea couldn't understand why all of a sudden Aggie was cool toward her and I couldn't really explain it to her - hell, I didn't understand it myself. But just as the good Doctor Frankenstein had created a monster, so had Aggie. Brea's first outing had merely whetted her appetite and now she wanted more. Since Aggie wasn't speaking to her anymore, she started going out by herself to pick up guys whenever her husband wasn't at home and she would always manage to get me out of earshot from Aggie and ask me to watch from the closet. Since Aggie was out looking for cock herself, I was usually able to say yes and Brea always thanked me by fucking my brains out. And then several bad things happened at once and my life turned to shit.

It was a Saturday night and Aggie was out on the prowl. The phone rang and it was Brea, "I've got someone I'm bringing home. Can you back me up in the closet?"

I looked at my watch and tried to judge Aggie's schedule. She would pick up one or two guys and do them in the parking lot of where ever she was before settling on one to bring home. I figured that she wouldn't be home until one, maybe two in the morning so I told Brea that

I'd be in her closet when she got home. An hour and a half later I'm in the closet watching some guy fuck Brea in the ass when the bedroom door opened and Brea's husband came in. He took one look at what was happening on the bed and then he went after the guy. Brea was screaming, the two guys were going at each other, the lover of the moment, trying to get out the door more than anything else, and then Brea did the one thing that I hoped and prayed she wouldn't - she came to the closet, opened the door and cried, "Stop them Dave, stop them!"

I was sitting in my apartment contemplating my navel and ruminating on the last two years of my life. Trying to separate Brea's husband and her lover got me seven stitches in my forehead and a broken nose. The fracas had worked its way out onto the front lawn and a neighbor had called the police. They managed to separate the three of us and then they took all three of us to jail.

When they let me out the next morning, I went home and found that all the locks had been changed. I banged on the door until Aggie came and told me to leave; that all further contact between us would be through her lawyer. A week later I was served divorce papers; I was being accused of committing adultery. Aggie wanted the house, the car, the savings and checking accounts and the credit cards. Given all that I had put up with from Aggie in the name of love, you would probably consider me a dumbass, but I can be surprising at times. When I was met by locked doors and talk of lawyers I immediately got my shit together. Within an hour I had changed all my credit cards to a "Mr. Only", I had changed the car door and ignition keys, and I was waiting outside the bank when it opened on Monday and I cleaned out the checking and savings accounts.

Again, love might have made me blind, but it hadn't made me stupid. I'd kept clear and concise records of all of Aggie's affairs over the past five years and I counter sued. The end result was a divorce that had us selling the house and splitting the proceeds sixty-six percent for me and the rest for Aggie and with Aggie having to pay for her own lawyer and court costs.

About a year later, Aggie tried to get back together with me, but I told her to "fuck off and die!" Brea and her husbands divorce was just as bitter as mine and Aggie's and Brea didn't come out of it very well since her husband was clearly the injured party. Luckily, none of us had kids.

The phone rang and I picked it up, "Hello? You bet. I love you too." I hung up and headed for the bedroom. I needed to be in the closet when Brea got home with her latest.

~The End~

Watch out for the next volume in Just Plain Bob's
Erotica Short Stories Series

Also by this Author:

From the Author

WANT FREE COPIES OF MY BOOKS?

Just visit my blog and download free copies of my books:
awesomeauthors.org/justplainbob

If you enjoyed any of my books then please share the love and promote my books in Amazon.

If you write me a review and send me an email I will send you a free book, or many.
(Just know that these emails are filtered by my publisher.)

Good news is always welcome.

One Last Thing, For Kindle Readers...

When you turn the page, Kindle will give you the opportunity to rate this book and share your thoughts on Facebook and Twitter. If you enjoyed my writings, would you please take a few seconds to let your friends know about it? Because... when they enjoy they will be grateful to you and so will I.

Thank You!

An Open Letter from Just Plain Bob

A message for those who like my stories, those who hate my stories, those who are indifferent and those who have yet to make up their minds.

I have often stated that I really don't care what others think about my stories, that I write for my own enjoyment and then I offer to share. If you like my stories fine and if you don't, also fine since I have already satisfied my target audience - me!

It is human nature to strive to get better. If you take up bowling your first games are going low scoring, but you will work and practice to get better and as your average climbs you may forget the game where you had three gutter balls and shot an eighty-six, but that game is still there in your past.

Your first time on the golf course you shot an eighty on the front nine, but did you settle for that being your game or did you work to improve? You may eventually get a three handicap, but that nine hole eighty is still there as part of your past.

When you hired in at your job did you say, "Cool, I got it made" and do nothing more than what you barely had to do or did you go to work thinking that, "Someday I'm going to be running this place." You might never climb that high, but human nature says that you are going to at least try.

It is the same with authors who write stories and post them on sites like Literotica. Their first stories might not be all that good, but comments and feedback along with a desire to get better drive them toward putting out a better product or to at least try.

I'm no different. My first stories might not have been all that great, but they are still there on the hard drive. I like cheating wife stories and five years ago I found my first adult site that catered to cheating wife stories. It was a pay site, but it had a policy of giving a free lifetime membership to anyone who submitted five stories to the site. How hard can that be I said to myself as I sat down and fired up the word processor and went to work.

I sent my five stories in and sat back to enjoy my free membership and a funny thing happened. I started getting feedback, most of it positive, and I became hooked. I started cranking out more stories. The site I was sending my stories to had seven categories:

Bisexual
Cream Pie

Groups
I Watch
Gang Bang
Racial
SM/BD

I know nothing about bisexual or SM/BD and I had no interest in Groups so all the stories I wrote I tailored for the four remaining categories:

Cream Pie
I Watch
Gang Bang
Racial.

I turned out eight stories a month, two for each category, which means that after five years I have over 120 stories in each of those categories and they are all still on the hard drive.

A year ago I received an email asking me why I never posted stories on Literotica. The answer? I didn't know about Lit. I pulled it up, liked what I saw, and started sending in stories to it. All new stories? No, not hardly, not with over 400 stories sitting on the hard drive. Maybe one new story for each fifteen or so old ones. The newer ones are better, at least I think they are and I have received some feedback that leads me to believe that others think so too, and I will continue to write new ones.

But I am still going to recycle what is on the hard drive, stories that were written specifically to fit the four categories. That means that those of you who hate cream pie stories still have eighty or so to look forward to. Ditto for those who call me a racist; you will get another seventy or so interracial stories.

Those who hate wimps will only see about fifty more of those because the stories I sent to the I Watch category were split 50/50 between what some call wimps and some call "real men." Why the 50/50 split? It came from listening to the readers. I would get feedback asking me why all the men in my stories were hard asses. "In real life men are more forgiving, especially if it is the first indiscretion." So I would write stories with forgiving husbands and boyfriends and then the next batch of feedback would say, "Why are all your husbands spineless wimps" and I'd write stories that went back the other way.

Eventually I came to realize that I was wasting my time - there was no way I could write a story that would satisfy everybody and that is when I adopted my philosophy of writing for my own enjoyment and then offering to share.

As far as the gangbang stories? Well, what can I say? Gangbangs are gangbangs and there are still eighty or so of them to go.

The bottom line is that Literotica readers are going to see more of my old stories than my new ones. If I'm still around three or four years from now it will probably go the other way, more new than old.

I feel the need to respond to some of the comments and emails I have received. By far the largest percentage comes from people who say, "You are an asshole because all women are not whores and sluts and that's all you make them out to be."

Next most common is, "You must really hate women you sick fuck."

"You must be a wimp because all the men in your stories are wimps" is up there in the top ten along with, "Why don't you give it a rest and go crawl off in a hole somewhere."

There is a lot more, but I'm only going to address those four and in reverse order.

I won't stop and go crawl in a hole because I am enjoying the hell out of what I am doing and remember what I said, I am doing this for MY OWN ENJOYMENT and then I offer to share. Some obviously like my sharing with them and so I will continue to do so. No one is holding a gun to a reader's head and telling them they must click on a Just Plain Bob story or die. It is a conscious choice on the reader's part to move that mouse and click on that story.

When a man finds out he has a cheating wife or girlfriend there are only a limited number of ways he can handle it. If he loves her he can forgive, try to forget and try to hold on and somehow make things work. He can turn his back on her, walk away and get on with his life. The third option is to take revenge.

According to a good portion of those who send me feedback the first and second options are proof that the men are wimps. If the man takes the third option he is still considered a wimp if he doesn't do some sort of physical damage to the woman and her lover. These readers believe that the only way not to be a wimp is to kill, maim and destroy everything in sight. Doing that however, will invariably get the man throw in jail and that is why it so rarely happens in real life.

In real life most revenge takes place in the man's head when he says to himself, "I should have _____ (fill in the blank) the fucking cunt!" I know this because I have been there and done that (see The Dark Trilogy). In my stories I try to mirror real life so kill, maim and destroy are going to be for the most part absent. Outside of some fisticuffs there will be very little physical violence in my stories. Most of my husbands are going to do what I did, what several of my friends and others that I know have done, forgive, or walk away. If this makes them wimps and me a wimp for writing the story that way, so be it.

Next is the "I must hate all women." Nothing could be farther from the truth. I love women. I lust after women. I even like whores and sluts. I have been married four times, engaged two other times (that did not end in marriage) and I have always had girlfriends between marriages. My philosophy is that women were put on this earth for me to enjoy and I'm not talking just sexually. I could sit at the mall (and have) for hours and just girl watch.

The engagements, girlfriends and three of the four marriages bring me to the #1 anti JPB comment on the list.

"You are an asshole because all women aren't whores and sluts."

Well dear reader, you can not prove that by me! I will say up front that I KNOW all women aren't whores and sluts, BUT the majority of the women in my life were. My mother ran around on my father for years while he was driving a truck for a living. My Aunt Margaret cheated regularly on my Uncle Bill, as did my Aunt Mildred on my Uncle Paul. My Aunt Betty fucked around on my Uncle Bob for years and finally left him for his brother, my Uncle Wendell. Uncle Wendell in turn caught her on her knees at his company Christmas party giving Season's Greetings to his boss.

My sister is three times divorced and each divorce came about when the then current husband caught her out spreading pollen. Both of the engagements I mentioned ended when I found out that I was not the one and only and a lot of the girls I dated between marriages never made it to engagement status for the same reason.

And that brings me to my three ex-wives. The first one, Helen (I believe I commented on her in the intro to The Dark Trilogy) had seven different lovers before I found out what was going on. I was living proof that love is blind. Ditto with my second wife. She had a secret life that she hid from me and when I found out about her brother, his friends and the gangbangs she was history.

My third marriage ended in divorce because of a different kind of cheating (and I can just imagine the outrage I am going to get over this) - she cheated on me with an idea. I was away from home on business, she was lonely, a couple of Jehovah's Witnesses knocked on the door and my wife, with nothing better to do invited them in. When I came home from my trip I found out that she had found God. On a scale that runs from TRUE BELIEVER on one end to ATHEIST on the other you will find me just to the right of AGNOSTIC and since I would not allow myself to be SAVED the marriage eventually died.

So yes, I write about sluts and whores because as everyone knows, you tend to write about the things you know. And I do like sluts and whores, just not the ones that lie to me and cheat on me.

So be forewarned - if you click on a Just Plain Bob story you will be getting sluts, whores and husbands who do not kill, maim and destroy. There are other things you will rarely find in a Just Plain Bob story. Even though I try to mirror real life my stories all take place in StoryLand. In StoryLand STDs and unwanted pregnancies do not exist unless the author feels like they may add something to the story. Bad things do not happen in StoryLand unless the author so wills it and no amount of "You should have..." in comments and feedback will change a story already posted.

Lastly, I will touch on a truth. None of what I have written here means shit because the same readers will still read the same stories that they profess to hate and make the same comments they have always made. Knowing this, I will deliberately post stories that will have them frothing at the mouth.

It is the least I can do for an adoring public.

Thank you!

Just Plain Bob
justplainbob@awesomeauthors.org

You may also like the books by these authors:

HOT EROTICA

HIRED FOR
Their Pleasure

A LATE BLOOMER'S 1ST TIME

JACK RYDER

"Mom was right, you have a gorgeous body," her voice startled me awake. I guess I must have stirred a bit when my body felt the pressure of someone sitting down on the bed next to me. I was still a bit groggy as I open my eyes to see Katie sitting there staring down at me. It took a few moments for to remember that I was completely naked. I instinctively reached to pull the blankets up but found that they had been kicked off onto the floor at some point in my sleep.

"Should I lock the door from now on, or is it acceptable for me to be naked every time you barge into my house unannounced?" My voice was hoarse and strained. I could see a look of lust on her face as she gawked at my flaccid prick. "You can be naked any time I come over," she told me with her eyes never leaving my dick. "Besides, Mom told you I would be over for breakfast." I glanced at the clock and it was ten after 9am.

"Do you think I'm pretty, Jake?" She whispered. "Oh hell yes, Katie...you are so very sexy," I told her as I felt a slight wiggle. Kathleen was wearing that tiny white bikini again. The way she was seated with one leg dangling off the bed and the other leg bent beside her, left her legs spread wide apart and I could see her pussy lips pressed tight against the crotch of her bottoms.

"But, I'm so skinny and I have no tits," she complained softly. "Even Stevie has bigger tits than I have," she lamented. "Are you kidding me?" I chuckled. "With that sexy slender body, those perky cone shaped tits are perfect." I gasped. "There are many men that prefer perky tits rather than the big globe type," I informed her. "You are incredibly sexy just the way you are, sweetie."

"Do you think you could like these as much as my mother's?" Katie reached up and untied her top so it fell forward to expose her breasts to me. "Ooooh Katie, look at you," I gasped as she reached back to undo the other string and her top fell off. Her small 32A cone shaped tits were less than a foot from my face. Her pink puffy nipples were exactly the same as her mother's but seemed more pronounced since her tits are more cone shaped. She also had those pure white triangles from her bikini tan line that has always aroused me deeply. "Damn, those are sexy," I gasped.

My dick had become fully rigid within seconds as I gazed at her exposed tits. "I see you're telling the truth," she giggled as she watched my dick bouncing against my belly. "You can touch them if you like," she whispered as she scooted a little closer and pulled her other leg up onto the bed. My hands were trembling noticeably as I reached forward to fondle both of her nubile little tits.

"That feels wonderful, Jake," she purred softly as she arched her back to press her breast firmly into my hands. I let go of her left breast and used placed my right hand around her waist so I could pull her forward. "Yes Jake, Yesssssss," she moaned as I wrapped my lips around her left puffy pink nipple and began to gently suck on it.

I felt her moving slightly and then felt her right hand wrapping around my rigid prick. "It's so big," she cooed when she saw that she could barely get her hand all the way around my girth. "Oooh, God Yes," I moaned as she started to gently stroke up and down my shaft. "So good, Jake, it feels s-o-o-o-o good," she gasped when I moved my mouth to suck on her other nipple.

My legs were quivering on the bed as she slowly jerked me off while I feasted on both of her perky tits. "I was so hard for you yesterday," I confessed as she got me closer and closer to orgasm. "You made my meat so wet when you were modeling those clothes," she answered me with a moan.

If you enjoyed this sample then look for **<u>Hired For Their Pleasure</u>**.

GEORGE X. BUSH

AFFAIRS Conundrum
ATONEMENT

WIFE SHARING EROTICA

John Rutter approached his front door very weary from his day's work. A last-minute meeting had pushed his day into overtime and at 8pm he was just getting home. As he entered, he was surprised to hear voices from within as he set his briefcase down. Walking into the living room, he was even more surprised to see his boss, Horace Ender, and his wife, Emma, along with the ubiquitous presence of Horace's bodyguard/right-hand man, Jared, all 6'8" and 275 pounds of sculpted black imperviousness. Even more jarring was the presence of Horace's secretary, Melissa, a 5'4" red-headed pixie with an upturned, freckled nose beneath bright green eyes.

"So, you're finally home," Jean, John's wife said, pressing her body into his and kissing him lightly on the lips. "Busy day?" she asked, her bright green eyes staring into his as her braless breasts rubbed lightly against his chest, her waist-length blonde hair swaying back and forth.

"Very," John replied, still wondering how he could have forgotten that everyone was coming over this evening.

"Sorry to surprise you, John," Horace said, at 65 still a silver-haired, energetic powerhouse of a man whose 6'3" frame was dwarfed by the presence of Jared standing behind him.

"Not at all," John replied, nonplussed. "I thought I had forgotten you were coming or something."

"Hello, John," Emma said, her silvery-grey hair tied back in a ponytail just like her husband's. At 63 and 5'6", Emma Ender was still a beautiful, willowy woman with bright blue eyes. "Nice to see you again."

"Emma," John replied, taking her hand and kissing her on both cheeks. "My pleasure. You look great," he said, admiring her and her husband, both very tanned from spending so much time at their home in Hawaii. "To what do we owe the pleasure?" he asked.

"Your future, John," Horace replied, a firm look on his face.

"My future?" John said a bit nervously.

"Yes," Horace answered. "Why don't you sit down and we'll talk," he said, indicating the large seat next to him.

As John settled nervously into the seat, everyone else settled down, too, Jean sitting between Melissa and Emma on the sofa while Jared stood behind John imposingly.

"Now see here, John," Horace began. "As far as your work goes, I can't say we've ever had a better, more productive employee, so rest assured on that score."

"I'm happy to hear it," John replied.

"Your energy, innovative thinking, and enthusiasm have all combined to bring in much business," Horace said. "So naturally we think of promoting you. We like to keep the best and the brightest and most promising at all costs."

"Wow, I don't know what to say," John said, truly surprised that this moment had come after only 2 years with the company.

"But we also consider other factors," Horace continued, "in deciding which people are worth keeping, factors such as honesty, morality, and suitability to our particular type of corporate culture. Being a productive worker just isn't enough anymore in today's marketplace."

"I understand," John replied.

"We're interested in determining whether you're such a person," Horace said. "But we do have some reservations, I must admit, which is why we're here tonight."

"What do you mean?" John asked, struggling to keep the nervousness from his voice.

"Well, we like to know that managers in our company are honest, truthful, and can be relied upon at all times, as well as whether they fit into our particular corporate culture," Horace said. "Are you such a person, John? Are you honest and truthful? Do you fully fit into our particular type of corporate culture? Can you be relied upon at all times to do what is required of you and do so with the utmost in discretion? Now, think before you answer. This is extremely important. Everything about your future with the company depends upon how you respond this evening."

Everyone just watched John expectantly, saying nothing. The tension was so thick you could cut it with a knife.

"The best answer I can give you," John replied after due consideration, "is that I always try to be honest and truthful. I'm not a saint and I don't always succeed, but it's important to me, too, so I try. As for being reliable and acting with discretion as far as the company is concerned, 150%," he stated. "I have to say that I've never had a job that was as challenging, yet as exciting and fun. I look forward to going to work each and every day."

"Yes, that we're well aware of," Horace said somewhat cryptically. "But we're referring to your entire life when we talk about honesty and truthfulness and integrity, and even to an extent our particular corporate culture. Was your answer only about work or did it also cover your life in general?"

"My life, period," John answered without hesitation.

"I see," Horace said, a disturbed look on his face.

"John, when we got married, we agreed to always be open and honest with each other, to share our lives completely," Jean said from her seat on the sofa. "No matter what."

"That's right," John agreed, nodding his head warily.

"Neither of us were virgins when we met, but I've been absolutely faithful to you ever since we got married," she continued.

"Can you say the same, John?" Emma asked quietly from the sofa.

John just stared at the three of them sitting there, realizing suddenly that both Melissa and Emma were each holding one of Jean's hands.

"No," John replied quietly after a minute. "I can't say the same."

"I'm glad you're being honest with us, John," Horace said after a few moments of pregnant silence filled the room. "That's very important, believe me. Now, you're saying you've been unfaithful to your wife; is that correct?"

"Yes," John replied, hardly daring to look Jean in the face but not daring to look anywhere else.

"Has it been one woman, many women?" Horace asked.

"Just one," John answered.

"I see," Horace said, nodding his head. "And was this a one-time thing or an ongoing thing?"

"It's been ongoing," John admitted, hating the look of pain in Jean's eyes as she stared at him, white-knuckled as she held Melissa & Emma's hands.

"Are you in love with this other woman?" Horace asked.

"No," John answered, exhaling a huge breath. "It's just sex, lust."

"Your wife doesn't please you, satisfy you sexually enough?" Emma asked softly.

"Oh, no, it has nothing at all to do with Jean," John exclaimed. "I'm totally, 100% committed to her. I love her. Our sex life is good, great. I never leave the house without..." he said, then stopped as he realized he was saying too much.

"Without what?" Emma asked, a smile almost creasing her face.

"Without, without..." John tried to say.

"Without fucking me," Jean filled in. "And when he gets home, that's usually the first thing that happens, we fuck. That's why I don't understand..."

"And if saving your marriage and your job, depended upon you stopping this behavior immediately, would you? Could you?" Horace asked.

"Yes," John replied emphatically. "My marriage and job are far more important to me."

"And you'd be willing to atone for your transgressions if need be?" Horace asked.

"Yes, if that's what's necessary," John said, nodding his head, feeling the sweat on his brow even though it was a cool evening and the windows were open.

"How shall you atone?" Horace asked almost rhetorically. "Is it possible to atone for this?" he asked, reaching down and picking up the remote control and pointing it at the television and pushing a button.

John stared in astonishment as a side-by-side picture of his office appeared on the television, one view being from the door, the other from the wall behind his desk facing the door. No part of his office was hidden from view.

"Shall we get started," John's voice came from the television, followed almost immediately by John himself with Melissa trailing...

If you enjoyed this sample then look for **Affairs, Conundrum, Atonement**.

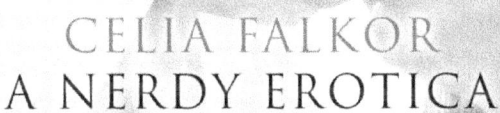

CELIA FALKOR
A NERDY EROTICA

DELECTABLE
COLLECTABLE

Stella heard Patrick knock on the bathroom door. "Can't I get a peek?" he pleaded.

She smiled and turned the lock, "I'm not ready yet. Be patient." Stella pulled up the zippers on her black boots and fastened the small, scalloped cape. Leaning forward, she examined her hair in the mirror. It was long, straight, and strawberry blonde.

But just to be sure that her bright mane looked top-notch, she ran a comb through it one last time. Then gingerly she put her mask on, hoping that its elastic band wouldn't push any stray strands in an ungainly direction. Glancing at the mirror again, she did a spin, making her black skirt billow beneath her yellow belt. Stella grinned, "Fabulous. Patrick?"

"Yeah honey?"

"Get ready for the reveal..." Unlocking the door, she opened it a crack and stuck one leg out, bending it sensually before kicking the door wide open. "What do you think?"

Patrick leaned against the wall, and let out a low whistle. "I don't think there'll be a sexier Batgirl found in the whole convention tomorrow."

Stella stepped up to him and gave him a light peck on the lips before running a finger along his shaved head. "Even if there was, I'm sure she'd be quite jealous of the strapping young man on my arm. Did the front desk have a catalog for the auction?"

"Yes."

"Well then, let's take a look."

"First you have to find it."

"Hide and seek?" Stella cracked her knuckles. "This shouldn't be too difficult." She turned and began an inspection of the hotel room, looking back at Patrick every so often to catch him staring at her bat-clad form. The catalog wasn't in or on the nightstand; wasn't under the bed, in the sheets, or among the pillows; and wasn't behind the TV or mini-fridge. "If you're going to enjoy the show, you might as well give me a hint."

"I can tell you that you're very cold."

"Am I?" Stella took a step toward Patrick.

"Now you're getting warmer."

Stella took a few more steps before standing nose-to-nose with him. "How warm am I now?" she whispered.

Patrick buried his face in her hair. "Red hot." Stella put one hand on his brawny chest and slid the other into his pants.

"Found it!" She pulled the rolled-up UltraCon catalog from its hiding place and hopped onto the bed. As she flipped through the glossy pages, Patrick lied down beside her and put his arm over her shoulder. Stella bit her lip as her eyes scanned the auction items listed, "Let's see... Section One: Props, Section Two: Costumes and Accessories, Section Three: Artwork, Section Four: Toys and Figurines..."

Patrick excitedly pointed to the bottom of one page, "There it is! Item 138!" The couple aimed a longing gaze at the catalog's listing: "Item 138, Princess Speer-La of Evermore figurine (with detachable skirt and spear). Limited Edition, 1982." Next to this was a photograph of the plastic princess.

She was six inches tall with long, Barbie-like hair and a painted-on leotard encrusted in ersatz jewels. She wore a silver skirt on her waist and in her right hand she wielded a spear the color of gold. "Mint condition," breathed Stella. Such preservation seemed like a miracle, given the nature of the toy's rarity. Only a thousand Speer-Las from the original line of Evermore toys had been distributed to retailers, and most of those were soon recalled when the princess's hewn cleavage sparked outrage among concerned parents.

Many of the remaining toys were discarded aimlessly by their child owners or hidden under mattresses by lusty, teenage boys. In the seven years that Stella and Patrick had been running their comic book shop, the Amazing Ashcan, they had heard of just a dozen Speer-Las still existing in the hands of private collectors. But in honor of UltraCon's twentieth anniversary, Mazda Mikkenson, the star of the 1985 *Speer-La* film, had donated her own Speer-La figurine to the convention's annual charity auction. Stella climbed onto Patrick's lap and held the open catalog in front of his face. "Where do you think it would look nice in the shop?"

"Hmmm..." As Patrick thought, his gaze wandered to Stella's bust, which was emblazoned with her costume's yellow Bat-symbol. "How about in a glass case above the counter? That way when people walk in, they can see my girl's hotter than the greatest warrior of Evermore."

Stella sat the catalog on the nightstand and turned to face him," And we can put another action figure in beside her, a stud that looks half as good as you..." She pressed her mouth onto Patrick's in a warm kiss, keeping her lips sealed even as she felt Patrick's tongue approach. He slid it along her upper and lower lip and across the seam of her mouth, poking at each corner to gain entry. His hands crept underneath her top and up to her strapless bra, where he pressed his palms against her covered breasts. Stella took a deep breath in, giving Patrick the opportunity to push his tongue into her mouth.

Her tongue laid in wait, and when they met they prodded at each other with a fury. Ripping from him and forcing his arms down, Stella began to unbutton Patrick's shirt. Once the last button had been freed, Patrick shook the shirt off and tossed it onto the floor. Stella began to lift her top off, but Patrick grasped her hands. "Not all the way. Here..."

He reached for the top's straps and flicked them off. Then slowly he pulled the top down until Stella's brassiere was on full display. Stella put one arm behind her back and unfastened the bra, which fell onto her lap. Taking one end in each hand, she flung the bra up and behind Patrick's neck like a lasso. Yanking him closer, she stuck out her chest, "You like these?"

"Yes." Patrick rasped.

Stella grazed her right breast against his cheek. "How much?"

"This much." He lifted Stella up off his lap and onto her back, laying his lower half onto hers while holding his torso up. His mouth closed in on one nipple…

If you enjoyed this sample then look for **Delectable Collectable.**

Step Desires

Backscratching Needs

Hot Taboo Erotica

I've always loved getting my back scratched. This is what would lead me into the steamy darkness of a wonderful, sensuous relationship with my stepmother in my adult life. That feeling of nice sharp fingernails dragged gently, softly down my back always soothed me, even when I was a child... even when I was quite an adult.

When I was a child, my mother used to scratch my back long and lovingly. It was one of my earliest memories. Mother died when I was only 7, and I have very few clear memories of her. But the feeling, that slow sensual scratching—softly, almost tickling—for long periods in the evening in front of the TV or the fire on cold nights, always reminds me of her.

I was nearing the end of 2nd grade when Mother had dropped me off at school. I was a bit late so I had to run inside, and missed the carnage when—pulling out onto the busy boulevard—Mother's little Toyota import was utterly crushed under a speeding cement truck. She was killed instantly. But her remains were in such a state that my father's identification of her body was something that traumatized and broke him forever. He would sometimes have flashbacks and nightmares years after. My entire young life was marked by tragedy.

Dad remarried. She was a woman who had been a family friend before her husband had run off, Jeanne Potter; she and I bonded almost instantly. Jeanne and Mom had been friends since high school. In her previous marriage, Jeanne and Dean Potter had a rough go of it. He drank and was a bit of a deadbeat. They had wanted kids, but she couldn't conceive—and he treated her badly because of it.

Jeanne had always adored me. As a close friend of my mother's, she had also been traumatized by her death—and had scooped me up the moment she heard the news. She picked up on my love of having my back scratched immediately. It helped soothe me through the loss of my mother. Perhaps it soothed us both. Dad and she were much thrown together after Mom's passing. They fell in love; maybe they had secretly been—who knows? My new stepmother, Jeanne Anderson, (she couldn't wait to take my father's name), was never a replacement for my real mother, but came an incredibly close second. At their wedding, I asked innocently if I could call her Mom. She had burst into tears and got down on her knees in her pretty white wedding dress and hugged me fiercely. It was never quite the same for her and my brother.

Jeanne, my new "Mom", and I have been thereafter always close—in a way that she wasn't with my brother. She and Dad had always had a very loving, affectionate relationship. I was more like her and Daniel was more like Dad. Not that my brother Daniel got along great with Dad, they were just more similar and had similar interests. They were into cars and sports. I was more into being quiet and reading, playing by myself when I got tired of the neighborhood kids. Jeanne had been like that, or so she told me.

Daniel was older than me by three years, but the age gap seemed much greater. There was no way he would ever allow his bookish younger brother to hang around with him and his friends. I didn't have lots of friends, but they were markedly different—bookish, nerdy, creative. Jeanne and my Dad worried a bit that we weren't closer, but had no idea how to make it better.

One spring, in my 18th year, they decided to take the family on a trip to the mountains of Colorado. Forced to be together, with no one else to hang out with, it was assumed we would bond a bit, being mainly in the great outdoors. Jeanne wasn't really into camping that much. Dad and Daniel were and often went camping, just the two of them. A few times, we had gone tent camping as a family, which was fun, but still not our favorite thing. This trip was to include a two night camp out in the wilderness. Not too wild, as you could drive right to the campsite.

Jeanne and I made camp while Dad and Danny went exploring. They had worked to get us to go, but the day was mostly gone and Jeanne wanted to start dinner. I had noticed the exquisitely cute girl two sites over and was more interested in her than humping it up to the falls. It was chilly out, being spring. The snow had only melted a month before and the river was flowing heavily. I started the fire while Jeanne started dinner. I set up the chairs and made a reasonably cozy campsite.

Afterwards I strolled up the bank of the river, mostly to get a closer look at the cute blonde with her hair pulled up into a sexy knot at the back of her head. She glanced over at me a couple of times as I passed, and her brilliant blue eyes made my heart pound. In a short time I was half a mile up the river. I sat in the slanting evening sunlight, at the edge of the pounding water, as the sun slipped lower and touched the mountains. I thought I had better head back as I had no flashlight if it got dark on me.

It was getting dark by the time I got back, expecting a telling off about being late for dinner. I strolled into the campsite and saw Jeanne/Mom sitting there alone by the dwindling fire, arms around her knees.

"Where did you get off to?" she asked, a slight edge to her voice. I told her that I was just up the river, watching the sunset. "Where the hell are your father and brother?" she asked no one in particular, her voice very edgy now. "They leave us to handle everything here, and simply head off by themselves. Plus, dinner is ready. It's getting cold!"

"We should just eat then," I told her, sitting in the chair next to her. "Let *them* eat cold food." She agreed and we did, sitting quietly munching chili and potato salad, pickles and garlic bread. "They're going to love this garlic bread cold," I muttered. Mom laughed. She asked me to clean our plates as she was going to set up her and Dad's bedding, and disappeared into the huge 12-man tent that we used for car camping.

I cleaned our plates and stuff by the glare of the Coleman lantern, and then went in and started setting up my air mattress and sleeping bag. I left Daniel's, rolled up by the side of the tent. We busied ourselves with these minor chores while we waited. We then went back to the fire and waited some more. Mom was really getting mad about them taking off and being gone so long.

"Did they take flashlights?" she finally asked. I told her that I didn't know. She seemed genuinely worried now, so I got up to check the stock in the box where all there lights were kept. They were all still there. I returned and told her so. "God damn it!" she swore exasperated. "Do you think they went way out and got stuck in the dark?" I agreed that it was possible, but reminded her that Dad was always prepared. He must have taken a small headlamp at least.

We sat by the fire awhile longer, adding logs and staying warm. "We could go look for them," I offered. Mom asked if I even knew which way they went. "Well, they headed up the river. I assume they were headed for the falls. Follow the river and we'll probably find them." She agreed. We sat a while longer. Mom kept looking over her shoulder up the river, as if expecting them to wander into the firelight any moment.

We sat there for another hour, chatting quietly about the trip so far, my relationship with my brother, school, that girl two sites over. She chided me over my shyness around girls and we both laughed a bit, but she was increasingly uncomfortable about Dad and Daniel being gone so long. I knew she was going to give them such a telling off when they got back.

"Should we go check with the rangers?" she wondered. I told her that the station was closed when I passed, but that they were probably cruising around. I would flag them down when they went by. We sat in silence now, staring into the flames. It was really getting late. Clearly, something was wrong. They must really be lost.

"I hope that none of them got hurt," she said quietly, sounding very distressed. Moments later the headlights from the ranger truck flashed on us as it approached. We both jumped out of our chairs. We flagged him down and explained the situation. He introduced himself as Ranger Mike and asked what time they had set out. We told him the time and he calculated that they would have just reached the falls at sunset, but that they would have passed the upper ranger station to get there. Perhaps it got too dark and they holed up there, he wondered. He got on the radio and called the ranger upriver, had he seen the two guys pass by? The ranger responded that he had and warned them that it was getting dark. His voice sounded irked that the yahoos had given him a 'Yeah, yeah, yeah.' reply and continued on.

Both rangers sounded a bit put out that now they had two people lost in the dark. They agreed that they would set out in the dark and go find them. Our ranger, Mike, told us to hang tight and wait for them to bring the guys in. We gave him their names and descriptions, and he headed off to arrange a search party, telling us to sit tight and not go anywhere. They didn't need more people going missing in the dark.

Mom and I returned to the fire to wait. Mom was really mad by now, but nervous at the same time. I could tell she was hoping that they were just lost, a stupid thing, and not hurt. She would give them such grief later.

By now it was midnight and we were both nodding off by the fire. "Screw this!" she said angrily. "I'm freezing. Let's go to bed. They can wake us up when they get back." She stood and marched to the tent, unzipping it roughly. I banked the fire a bit and followed. I went in and turned to zip it closed. Mom stood there staring at the two sleeping bags that she had zipped together for her and Dad. "Well, your father isn't here to keep me warm, so why don't you climb in with me?" It wasn't really a question.

I watched as she quickly tossed off her jacket and shucked off her jeans. She was wearing silk long johns, top and bottom, and pulled a Flashdance move, unhooking and removing her bra from underneath her shirt…

If you enjoyed this sample then look for **Step Desires**.

EROTIC ROMANCE

MOLLY'S
Daughter

LILITH JONES

After the lunch crowd had gone, Anne Bernard watched Mom from the window of the diner until she got to the house. Minutes later, Mom called that she was lying down.

Mom had handled the diner for years by herself. Anne hadn't appreciated how much work it was. Even when she had helped after school, she had bitched at how hard she worked instead of seeing the killing hours Mom had worked. And, then, she'd left Mom to handle it herself for three school years while she was in college. Mom had lied to her about the cancer when she was home for Christmas, though she could tell Mom wasn't feeling healthy.

Now, Mom still came in for lunch and dinner hours. It was Molly's Diner, and Molly still kept it up.

-=-

Greg Thibault shook the cell phone in his hand. He kept from throwing it across the mesa by telling himself that that would only make the situation worse. And a worse situation than the present would be unbearable. Every arrangement which had been "of course, Professor Thibault," or "no problem, Greg," when he had been in Boulder was unraveling at the other end of an unreliable connection.

"Look," he said, "I'll call you back in an hour or two with better reception." He punched off. He didn't know whether the guy at the department had heard him, but they would know that he wasn't on the line.

The phone companies boasted that they covered 99% of the people living in the country. This mesa was in the 1%. To be fair to the phone companies, not that Greg felt like being fair to any phone companies right then, the Anasazi weren't actually *living* in the United States. The last of them had been dead five centuries now.

He gave elaborate instructions to his students, descended by the footpath, and headed out in his Jeep. He took a quarter hour to get to something paved. The Jeep was supposed to be an off-the-road vehicle. It's just that the mesa was further off the road than the Jeep had been designed for. He found that his AC was dead, but he would have to climb back up the mesa and down again to get the keys for another vehicle. He opened the windows and got hot, moving air.

He wondered vaguely just why he'd bothered with giving the directions. Being a programming executive described as "like herding cats." Supervising archeological graduate students was like that, but worse. Everybody knew how to do the job better than the instructor did.

The nearest cellphone tower was between the two small towns of Randolph and Copper City. Randolph, the closer one, was more than an hour away. Even so, he passed only three cars on his way. Archeology got done in dry, empty country. It wasn't that Minnesota hadn't had cultures living in the area for millennia; it was that most of their artifacts had rotted or sunk into the ground. When the Anasazi had tossed out a potsherd, it was still where they'd tossed it.

He pulled into the parking lot of a diner in Randolph and called again. His hassles had only begun, and he spent half an hour on the cell, mostly on hold. By then, sweat was running down his body and pooling in the seat of his pants.

Hot, still air was worse than hot, moving air. And the air down here was, if anything, hotter than the air on the mesa. He looked across at Molly's Diner. He had seen the air conditioner when he'd driven in. His glasses were too streaked with his sweat now, but he could hear it when he listened. He'd been an idiot. He would go in and ask to make the other calls from there.

He'd left before lunch. He hadn't missed much. Assigning cooking duties only to coeds would be arrant sexism. On the other hand, guys who were going to major in Anthro didn't take home-ec in high school. Most girls who were going to major in Anthro didn't take home-ec either. Or, if his present students had, they had forgotten everything they'd learned in that course.

The diner had an air conditioner. He could hear it. He'd eat and make the rest of his calls from there. He headed into the diner.

-=-

Anne didn't recognize the customer who came in. The non-local customers were truckers. How had an 18-wheeler got into the lot without her hearing it? The guy looked rugged, but not like a trucker, and she didn't know why for a minute. Then she did. He was tanned, deeply tanned, but the tone was even. Truckers had more tan on the left side.

She grabbed a menu, and the guy sat at the counter. She got behind the counter and handed him the menu. He took off his glasses and held the menu close.

"The home-made chile looks good," he said. "Might I have some of that?"

"Coffee?"

Greg shivered, and it wasn't the AC. That voice was the sexiest voice he'd ever heard. And she wasn't trying to be sexy. She had only asked if he wanted coffee.

"Please."

Anne poured him his coffee before getting the chile. Truckers, and many locals, were more interested in the coffee than in the food. She'd learned to brew good coffee. That meant pouring out a lot and alternating pots and scrubbing them often. A cup of coffee brought in more than making a pot cost, though, and truckers chose to stop based on the quality of the coffee.

Greg liked the coffee. The chile was the best-tasting food he'd had since he'd come to the mesa. Better than that, it tasted good. He got a napkin out of the dispenser and wiped off his glasses. The waitress was the sexiest woman he'd ever seen. And it was neither her attitude nor her clothes.

She was wearing a blouse that covered her to the elbows and an apron over that. He'd spent the last two weeks with girls wearing shorts and halters, and none of them had been so attractive. The waitress had long hair, but it was tied up in a bun with a pencil stuck in it.

She hadn't presented the bill, but he paid with a $20. She brought him back his change. She stayed within sight while he ate, and that was easy on the eyes.

"Look, ma'am," he said, "the air is out in my Jeep. I have some calls to make from this area. I've been working in a dead zone." He held up his cell. "Would you mind if I made them from that table back there?"

Anne said, "Go right ahead. Want more coffee?"

"Please." This guy had said please more often to her in the last ten minutes than some regular customers had in the last month. She couldn't figure him. He didn't have a local accent. Something in his speech reminded her of the professors at Tempe, though they hadn't been that polite. He looked like he sweated every day in the sun, and he sounded like he spent his life in a library.

He stood at the counter until she had refilled his cup. Then he carried it to a table by the door. By the air conditioner, too, she noticed.

He talked on his cell. He'd been right that he had *some* calls to make. After the second, he drained his cup and put it down. She carried the pot to his table to refill the cup.

"You didn't have to do that," he said. "I could have gone back for it."

"I wait tables."

"And cook?"

"And sweep the place out at night," she said. "This place barely supports Mom and me. It couldn't pay for a big staff." How barely it supported them, she wasn't going to tell a stranger, however nice he talked.

"Well, I don't know about the sweeping, but if you cooked that chile, you did a damned fine job."

"Why, thank you."

A trucker came in for coffee and pie just then, and she didn't pay attention to the guy until the trucker was served. The guy got loud on the phone towards the end, though, and she could hear that. Apparently, he could tell.

"A lady can overhear me, which puts a real crimp in my vocabulary. But you can take the next down handbasket." The person at the other end apparently said something. "No. Both of you are women, but only one is a lady."

After he closed the cell, he brought his cup to the counter for more coffee and ordered a hamburger. He waited there for the burger, paid, and waited for his change. The driver went out and the guy went back to his table. He made another call and argued some more.

Greg was perfectly well aware that yelling on the phone didn't make them hear you any better. Sometimes, though, he couldn't resist. Finally, he ended his last conversation with Boulder and closed the cell. He brought his cup and saucer back to the counter.

"What sorts of pie do you have?"

Anne said,"Peach, apple, and cherry. We don't cook the pies, though." She couldn't figure why she'd said the last. Just that the guy had said nice things about the chile.

"I'll risk some cherry, anyway. And more coffee." She got the coffee and the pie. He paid immediately, using some of the change she'd given him earlier. She suddenly wondered whether the $20 bill was all the money he'd brought with him.

Greg ate the pie slowly. He told himself that he wanted to stay because of the coolness. The waitress was great to look at, and great to listen to, though she hardly spoke to him. Still, she was a pretty girl in a town full of young men. She was certain to be taken. He could look, but not touch.

"You were right," he said, pushing an empty plate and an empty cup away. "The pie was not home cooked. Nothing wrong with it, though. This is a nice place, how long are you open?"

That, he thought, was real suave, Thibault, not! 'When do you get off?' Indeed. The question isn't when she gets off, but where you get off.

"We're open six to ten."

"Thanks." He put a couple of bills under the edge of his plate and walked towards the door. "Really, thanks for everything," he said before going out. It would be a long drive back, and into the setting sun, too.

Anne said, "You're welcome," in a voice which was probably too low for him to hear. Then she got his dishes, spoon, and fork into the soaking water. There wouldn't be many customers before supper. She might as well wash the dishes now, so she did.

She put the tip into the cash register. About half the truckers and a quarter of the locals tipped. Their tips seldom folded. Of course, the guy had eaten a lot, and he had asked about making calls from here. But people called on cells from the diner all the time. Two free refills weren't a lot, and he sure hadn't made her walk. She did hear his car leave, though she hadn't heard it arrive.

Well, she'd tell Karen about the mysterious stranger in September, and she would invent one of her marvelous stories to explain him. Then Anne stopped smiling.

Would she go back to school in September? Would she ever see Karen again?

If you enjoyed this sample then look for **Molly's Daughter**.

WANT FREE COPIES OF MY BOOKS?
Just visit my blog and download free copies of my books:
awesomeauthors.org/justplainbob